REDEMPTION
in the
MONARCHY
BATHSHEBA
Daughter of the Oath

REDEMPTION *in the* MONARCHY

BATHSHEBA
Daughter of the Oath

Kari Mann

XULON PRESS

Xulon Press
2301 Lucien Way #415
Maitland, FL 32751
407.339.4217
www.xulonpress.com

© 2019 by Kari Mann

All rights reserved solely by the author. The author guarantees all contents are original and do not infringe upon the legal rights of any other person or work. No part of this book may be reproduced in any form without the permission of the author. The views expressed in this book are not necessarily those of the publisher.

Unless otherwise indicated, Scripture quotations taken from the Holy Bible, New International Version (NIV). Copyright © 1973, 1978, 1984, 2011 by Biblica, Inc.™. Used by permission. All rights reserved.

Printed in the United States of America.

ISBN-13: 978-1-54566-607-4

To Denise
A prayer warrior who's pioneering efforts
in publishing her prayer journals made me
believe in myself with this Old Testament tale.
I value our friendship.

INTRODUCTION

Samuel held a fistful of dirt in his palm as he crouched in the meadow outside of Jerusalem. A few days ago, the Lord had instructed him to tell King Saul, because of his rejection of God's commands, God had now rejected him as king over Israel. Samuel wiped the dust from his hands as he stood. God now called Samuel to travel to a little hamlet known as Bethlehem on the road due south. He remembered when he first began following in the Lord's leading; he was just a teen.

Samuel had been living with Eli, the priest. His mother Hannah had suffered for years with a barren womb. In a culture where children were thought to be one of God's greatest blessings, the inability to have children must be a judgment from Jehovah himself. Samuel listened to the shuffling of his own feet as he allowed his mind to wander back into his childhood. Hannah promised God that if He would give her a son, she would return her son to God for His service. Old Eli had spotted her crying and carrying on in her anguish. Years later he would apologize to Samuel–"I thought she was drunk!"–when she was simply pouring her heart out to God.

"In that case," Eli had responded, "Go in peace and may God grant your request."

God responded indeed! God opened Hannah's womb and gave her a son; *me*! Samuel chuckled to himself and looked up to the sky. 'Was this your will all along, Jehovah? That you would choose me, Samuel, as your humble servant and voice to your people?'

As a boy, Eli had taught him all about serving as a priest of the nation of Israel. Then one night, there was that voice that called him by name. Samuel had assumed that it was Eli and remembered that he was a bit annoyed that the old man was calling him out of a deep sleep but dutifully answered. Eli claimed it wasn't him so Samuel returned to his slumber. The voice called out again. Puzzled, Samuel still thought it to be his mentor and again, answered back; ready to serve. A second time, Eli denied that it was his voice that Samuel heard. This happened a third time when it must have dawned on Eli who was calling Samuel. Eli had instructed him that it was the Lord calling.

Samuel looked up toward the sun and squinted. He put his hand over its brightness and watched a falcon cross the sky as he continued in his reverie. He could see Bethlehem in the distance and wanted to pick up his steps so he would get there before sundown. He had to pause and leaned on his walking staff as a teenage shepherd led a herd of sheep across the road toward a nearby well. The bleating of the animals and the barnyard stench were common in this area. Bethlehem produced many of the livestock used in Jerusalem's temple worship. Samuel hadn't been much older than that shepherd boy and he certainly hadn't known the Lord when he lived with Eli; he was just a willing servant, ministering to the people. When Eli told him that it was God calling — the audible voice of God — calling to *him*, Samuel remembered that he didn't quite know what to expect. As instructed, when he heard the voice call him by name a fourth time, he answered, "Here I am."

Chuckling to himself, Samuel thought 'and here I still am. I have grown old but the years have flown swiftly as I have faithfully served as God's voice to His people.' His brow furrowed as he acknowledged that being a prophet is not an easy life. Eli's sons were scoundrels. They did not take the role of priests seriously. They were enterprising and selfish, using their position for personal gain. The Lord decided they would not succeed the priesthood after Eli, so it had fallen to Samuel.

"Dear Lord, I have tried to let none of your words fall to the ground." Samuel prayed aloud. "You have blessed Israel by giving them ears to hear. I have boldly gone and told King Saul of your displeasure." 'And here we are again.' Samuel thought. King Saul has turned into quite a scoundrel as well. Who shall succeed him?

Bethlehem. That was where God told him to go. A man named Jesse with many sons lived there. Samuel focused on the dirt path ahead of him. When he finally arrived in the small town, the elders of Bethlehem met him.

"It's the prophet Samuel!" One cried out loud.

"Do you come in peace?"

"Why have you traveled to Bethlehem?

"Lord, God, have mercy on us!"

They all spoke at once, in worried tones and with trembling fear. This was the price of being a prophet. No one was excited to see you, for they assumed you never came with good news. Samuel held up his weary hands and put them at ease. "I have come to sacrifice to the Lord. Could you please lead me to the house of Jesse?"

When they arrived at Jesse's home, the elders joined in the sacrifice Samuel offered to the Lord with Jesse.

"I was told to come to you by God. Please introduce me to your sons for one of them will be chosen by God to lead Israel."

Jesse exchanged a gasp and incredulous expressions with the elders. A man of leadership from Bethlehem? This man was one of his sons? Jesse took a few steps toward his house, clapped his hands and began to call his sons by name. Servants scattered to go fetch them. Abinadab passed in front of Samuel and the old prophet thought, 'surely the Lord's anointed stands before me.' He paused a moment, listening for God's direction. Samuel shook his head; God told him, no. This was not the chosen one.

Jesse then had his second oldest son, Shaman, pass by but again Samuel waved him by. "No, the Lord has not chosen this one."

Eliab. No, he is not the one.

Nethanel. No, God has not chosen him.

Radii. Ozem. Elihu. Seven of Jesse's sons passed by Samuel and the Lord's response each time was clear. This was not the man. Samuel sat for a moment, weary. The elders, Jesse and the brothers all stood awkwardly nearby as the prophet bowed his head in silent prayer.

Samuel began to speak words that the Lord was giving him. "Do not consider how a man looks or how tall or how short he is as a reason I have rejected him. I do not look at the outward appearances, says the Lord, but I look at the inner workings of a man's heart." Samuel looked at Jesse. "Do you have any more sons?"

Jesse pointed off over some hills. "There is the youngest, but he is out tending our herds of sheep." The brothers exchanged knowing looks as if to say, 'yea–he is of no consequence.'

"Send for him." Samuel instructed. "We will not sit down until you return with him." He pounded his walking staff in the dirt for emphasis and some of the brothers who had sat down, stood back up. Jesse looked around, from his sons to the elders, and then ran off to find his youngest son.

Moments later, Jesse arrived with a teenager. Samuel noticed the boy was in good health, had strong muscles and handsome features. Even though God had specifically said that He does not look at the outward appearance but the inner heart, in this case–the lad had it all.

"What is your name?" Samuel asked him.

"David." The boy responded and lowered himself on one knee, bowing in respect to the prophet Samuel. Samuel smiled. God's word came to him loud and clear and he was happy to share it with the crowd.

"This is the one. I will anoint him." Samuel fumbled at his waist for the horn of oil that he brought with him. In the presence of his brothers, father Jesse and the elders of Bethlehem, a boy named David was chosen by God. The Spirit of God came powerfully upon David that day.

Samuel raised his hands in worship, giving thanks for the provision of God. Bethlehem had produced the next king of Israel. Samuel looked up to the vast sky and his mouth opened in awe. The continued words of God were given to him by the Spirit, but Samuel was instructed not to share them with Jesse or David at this time. David's house would indeed be mighty. His reign would be remembered for generations, but it would also be marred by the sword. For reasons Samuel would never know, the sword would never leave the house of King David. Another innocent lamb would be sacrificed at the hand of this mighty, chosen king when he allowed his own selfish desires to cloud his vision. Samuel cocked his head as if he could audibly hear the voice of God that was ringing in his head. A woman, like his faithful mother Hannah, would play a significant part in this great monarchy. Jehovah, in his infinite mercy, would provide another prophet like Samuel to walk alongside David as he travels this dark path of his own iniquity and bring blessing and good out of circumstances that are dark and sinful.

Samuel would never have the privilege of meeting Nathan this side of heaven, but they were kindred spirits. He bowed his head and sent a prayer up to God to give this other prophet wisdom and humility for such a task. The life of a prophet is not an easy one. Looking into the hopeful eyes of a teenage David, Samuel's eyes welled with tears. 'It is also not easy being a king. May God be with you.' Samuel thought as he kissed the top of David's head, full of tousled hair. He smelled like the herd of sheep Samuel had encountered on his journey to Bethlehem. The oil of his anointing still ran down David's cheeks.

"And now, O Lord." Samuel began to speak. "You have promised good things for this servant. May it please You to bless his house and his wife, their sons and their son's sons." Samuel would never see it come to pass, but God's promise rested on David's son, the future King Solomon. Ultimately, in generations to come, the greatest King mankind would ever know will be from the house of David. The annals of scripture would record this legacy of Israel, God's chosen people.

"The Lord declares that He himself will establish a house for you. When your days are over and you rest with your ancestors, I will raise up your offspring to succeed you, your own flesh and blood and I will establish his kingdom. He is the one who will build a house for My name and I will establish the throne of his kingdom forever."

But it wouldn't stop there. Another ruler would follow Solomon, one greater and eternal, and would be born here in the insignificant sheep town of Bethlehem.

"But you, Bethlehem Ephrathah,
though you are small among the clans of Judah
out of you will come for Me

> *One who will be ruler over Israel,*
> *those origins are from of old,*
> *from ancient times."*

As Samuel shuffled away from the house of Jesse, he paused and turned back. He watched the sun dip low and almost touch the tops of the nearby hills. 'A woman.' The thought crossed his mind again. 'A woman will play a significant role in this kingdom.' Samuel smiled wearily and nodded as he turned on the road back to Jerusalem, leaving Bethlehem behind. God's ways are not like our own. If there is one thing Samuel had learned, serving his entire life as a prophet, he knew this to be true. Just like this shepherd boy that God picked to be the next King of Israel after Saul. 'I would have gone with the eldest, Abinadab.' Samuel thought to himself. But God didn't ask Samuel what he thought, just for his obedience. 'I bet this woman of significance will wonder why God didn't ask her what she wanted in life either.' Samuel thought grimly. 'But I also hope that she trusts God enough to know that He is good and will work all circumstances *for* His good . . . even if they don't make sense or feel good at the time.'

CHAPTER ONE

B athsheba quietly stroked the *kallah* veil she would soon wear on her head. Her fingers traced the carefully stitched hem as her mind wandered. Had it been a year? She had been filling the water jugs down at the well and hadn't noticed him when she walked back into her father's home all those months ago. But there he stood. Tall and handsome. He was shaking hands with father and the two men turned when she had entered the house. They had agreed upon a *mohar;* a price for her to be his bride. How her stomach had fluttered. She had quickly put the water jars down on the dusty floor before she dropped them as her hands began to shake. How quickly her life was going to change. She was betrothed.

What a man of prestige had Jehovah chosen for her to be her bridegroom! His name meant "God is my light" and seemed to live up to his namesake. He had warm eyes that viewed her with such kindness. Uriah was part of the Hittite minority in Israel when he came to live in the land of the tribe of Simeon in the southern region of Israel which her family was a part of. He had been stationed there as part of a remote outpost of King David's army and was planning to return to Jerusalem upon the completion of their wedding.

Bathsheba noticed that her hands bore some callouses and small wounds from the months she and her mother had been sewing the wedding garments and veil. She looked over at the small table where she and her mother had been preparing the wedding cakes. There sat the beautiful oil lamp and and necklace that Uriah had given her as wedding gifts. She would be well cared for as the wife of a military officer, but she was not looking forward to living so far away from her family. She gathered her tunic as she sank onto a nearby stool and began to play with her chestnut hair. What would it be like to be a wife?

"Good morning, my daughter." Her father, Eliam walked in, shaking her from her daydreaming. "The sun is setting, soon your groom will arrive!" He pronounced it proudly like when the goat had produced the jug of milk last spring. Bathsheba nodded, not trusting the quiver in her throat to produce audible sound. She had not seen Uriah for a week, as was Jewish custom. If only she could see his face she knew he would be able to calm the flutter she felt. Her mother flew in the room, clapping nervously.

"Come! It is time for your *mik'vot*. You must purify yourself for tonight. Your attendants are waiting at the baths."

Bathsheba obediently rose from the stool and followed her mother out into the pasture to a small hut with a water basin. It was already filled with water with a few purple saffron floating on the surface. She smiled as she immersed herself into the bath and allowed herself to be washed by her attendants who were chattering excitedly about the nightly events. Weddings were always an exciting occasion for the town. She had attended many of these celebrations for friends and tonight it was her turn to be the bride. The excitement was contagious.

"When God created Adam as the *Talmud* teaches, He could not contain all of His attributes in a single human. So He created Eve and upon their union as husband and wife, the reunification of there two parts become one." Bathsheba's mother cupped her daughter's face in her weathered hands and smiled. Bathsheba drank in the maternal love and smiled back. "Soon, my daughter, you will be joined with your husband as God designed."

Bathsheba was finishing getting dressed into her gown by candlelight when she heard a baritone shout from outside the house walls. He was here! She skipped to the front room of the house and waited expectantly for him to open the door. She adjusted the veil on her head. Her four attendants stood behind her giggling nervously, holding hands, waiting for the procession to begin; Martha, her childhood friend from town, her sisters Sarah and Miriam, and Deborah, her mother's cousin. They had been her confidants, her companions as she made the transition from childhood into womanhood. It was fitting they were here to celebrate with her on her wedding day. Her parents appeared together at her left, also looking anxiously toward the door. Elaim, her father was holding the *Kesubah*, the marriage contract he had written with Uriah that listed all the responsibilities that would be transferred from father to husband to care for Bathsheba. Her older sister, Ziva and her husband Jacob would serve as the escorts. The were already holding their candles and symbolize joy with their warm glow. The world grew still and quiet. She felt a little sad to be saying goodbye to her father's house that had been her home all these years. She quickly glanced around the simple room. There was nothing left of hers. It had all been packed and taken to the home Uriah had prepared for her. There was no place for her in her father's house.

She heard the sound of a *shofar* horn and the door suddenly opened with a bang. She released a nervous chortle and watched her attendants beginning to bounce a bit. Uriah stood at the doorframe with his arm outstretched for her. He wore his *kittel*, a white linen robe to indicate his spiritual readiness for marriage. His attendants and a few wedding guests were outside the door peering over his shoulder to get a peek at the bride.

"Bathsheba!" He called to her joyfully. She was surprised at how readily her heart responded to his call. Just moments ago, she had been melancholy about closing the door on adolescence. Her heart liked how he said her name. Now, she knew in her heart that her home was now with her husband. He was a loving man, good provider and she found herself anxious to please him. She quickly put her hand in his and with a laugh, he led her out the door.

They were immediately surrounded by friends and family who had come to wish them well. The air filled with cheering, laughter and the clamor of celebration. The crowd parted a bit, and Uriah and Bathsheba led the crowd, hand in hand for a procession to the *Huppah*, the bridal chamber that Uriah had been preparing all these months. It was a few houses away, borrowed lodging where Uriah was staying until their move to Jerusalem.

In the courtyard, Bathsheba saw the *chuppah* canopy come into view. It symbolized a home and in moments, she and Uriah would stand beneath it before the rabbi. He squeezed Uriah's hand a little more tightly. Twilight was replaced by candlelight as Bathsheba released Uriah's hand and was taken by her escorts, Ziva and Jacob. She was led around Uriah seven times to represent the seven days of creation as the rabbi began reading the seven marriage blessings.

"Blessed are you, God of the universe who creates the fruit of the vine. Blessed are you, God of the universe who created everything for His glory. Blessed are you God of the universe who forms mankind. Blessed are you, God of the universe who formed man in His image and physical form." Bathsheba silently took her place beside Uriah under the canopy. Rachel and Jacob melted into the crowd of people that surrounded them as her mother stepped forward with a cup of wine. Assisting Bathsheba with her veil, she helped her to take a sip as the rabbi continued with the blessings.

Uriah's friend in the military, Beneniah served as his best man. He produced a wine glass that was carefully wrapped in white cloth and placed it under Uriah's foot. Triumphantly, Uriah stomped on it and the sound of tinkling glass as it shattered caused the on-lookers to celebrate with joyful shouts. Bathsheba had been taught this tradition was to symbolize the marriage bed. The newlyweds turned from the canopy and walked to the home Uriah prepared. The doorway had been decorated with grapevines, water lilies and saffron. He opened the door and ushered her in. She turned just in time to see the smiles of her parents as they discreetly turned away to prepare the wedding feast while she and Uriah had a moment of privacy.

He closed the door behind them and stood looking at her. The world grew quiet once more. He was smiling, but did not seem to be in a hurry. She was thankful for that. As excited as she was to learn how to be a good wife, she was nervous about consummating the relationship. Especially knowing all those people were waiting outside to begin the wedding feast. He motioned for her to sit on a bed he had covered with wool blankets and down pillows. He sat beside her and clasped his hands in his lap.

"Bathsheba." Her heart leapt as he said her name. "I have looked forward to this night when we would truly become one in the eyes of Jehovah. You are a beautiful and righteous woman. I have admired you so for many, many months." He shyly looked down. "I sound like I am reading from a script. I feel like a giddy schoolboy!" He looked back into her eyes and kissed them. "You looked so beautiful under the canopy just now. Your eyes reflected the candlelight." She smiled. "It was such a beautiful ceremony. I am so thankful to God for giving me such a wonderful woman for a wife! How was you day?"

Bathsheba giggled. He was concerned with the happenings in a woman's life? "Yes, thank you. Mother and I finished packing my trousseau this morning and my attendants cheered me all day."

"That is well." He smiled. He took her face in his hands. They were gentle and strong. He gently kissed the top of her veil near her forehead. His hands slid to her shoulders and worked the tunic down her torso. Bathsheba could barely breathe. How wonderful a night was this? All the poetry she had read as a child would blossom into reality here on her wedding night. The act was so strange and yet so intimately connected her to her husband, she silently gave thanks to Jehovah for his provision.

They laid together afterward in the darkness for a moment. The guests outside were stirring a bit, she could hear them clinking the pottery and could smell the roast on the fire. Uriah held her hand and said a prayer of gratitude to the Lord as well. With her veil still in place, they prepared to open the *Huppah* door and rejoin their guests. Uriah was folding the virginity cloth for her father and tucked it under his arm as he held the other out for her to grasp his hand once more. He winked at her before opening the door. Bathsheba knew it was one of many secrets the two of them would share in the years to come as the walked life together as husband and wife. Their guests greeted them with an eruption of shouts and laughter that signaled the wedding feast may commence. Uriah stood before her and removed her veil for the guests to see her face. She was smiling radiantly. Two relatives and her father, Eliam stepped forward to receive the virginity cloth from Uriah and in turn, Uriah signed the prepared *Kesubah* marriage contract. She watched as he handed it to her with as much respect as if he was handling the Torah. The men huddled in a circle as the cloth was unfolded. The tradition was for Bathsheba's honor. The cloth was physical proof of a blood spot indicating the hymen membrane of the virgin bride had indeed been broken on the wedding night. The men nodded in consent. Uriah had kept his bride pure until this moment and the wedding was witnessed and made official. Her mother and her aunt took the cloth from her father and refolded it. She walked with her mother to her wedding trousseau that was nearby and placed it along the other belongings for safekeeping.

"Uriah," her father commanded the ear of all the guests as he placed a paternal hand on his shoulder. "She is your wife now. You have fulfilled you *mohar* obligations as bridegroom to me, her father. May Jehovah keep you safe as you journey home, send you many children and may you walk with Him all the days of your life." The guests clapped and Uriah led Bathsheba to their place at the feast table. They took cups and toasted them together.

Bathsheba tore a large peace of braided bread as dancing got underway. She clapped and watched her guests celebrate their marriage to the lively music. She exchanged smiles with her mother who was watching her from across the room. She made a point to thank Ziva and Jacob for serving as her escort and to encourage her younger sisters as they imagined their own canopies and grooms one day. As she hugged and greeted her guests, a warm breeze kicked up and blew out some of the candles. Out of the corner of her eye, she caught her father catching a corner of a tablecloth that was dangerously dancing near one of the candles. For a split second, Bathsheba's joy was replaced by childish worry of doom. Was the a bad sign? Uriah's laugh brought her back to reality. This was her marriage reception, a joyful night. She was his wife at last. It was the start of a wonderful life together. What could spoil that?

CHAPTER TWO

Time passed swiftly. Bathsheba had been a wife for nearly several months now. Uriah had brought her to Jerusalem where they lived in one of the many wings of the royal palace. Their wedding seemed as distant as the hometown she had left behind. Uriah was a wonderful man that she had grown to love deeply. He was a man of integrity. He feared the Lord and held his position in King David's army as one of the Mighty Men. This group of thirty warriors was significant and spoke of his honorable reputation in the city. She had become friendly with Anna, Benaiah's wife, another great warrior who served alongside Uriah as the King's bodyguards within the army and who had served as Uriah's best man. The two women would comfort each other when King David's many conquests would call their husbands away to the battlefield. King David would often confide in Uriah and Benaiah and they were also close to the Lord's prophet, Nathan. The men would meet together regularly to assist Nathan in charting the histories of King David's reign and getting the details written down accurately. Bathsheba enjoyed the times when she was allowed to listen to the oral renditions of what the Lord had done in the life of their king.

Bathsheba placed a bowl of soup down in front of Uriah for dinner. He looked especially tired tonight. The sun had begun to set, painting the sky many shades of orange, reminding her of summer squash and her father's home where they had grown that squash in the garden so many months ago. The memory made her smile.

"How was your day?" He asked after blessing the food. Bathsheba smiled. Ever the gentleman who cared about how she spent her hours. She told him about the busy marketplace, how she had found the spice for the lamb for the Sabbath and the progress she was making on the wedding blanket for a friend. He nodded, distracted with the burdens of the day. She touched his arm, causing him to look up from the bowl of soup into her eyes. He smiled. She knew him so well. He carried himself in the city with such assertive confidence. Supported his king and God and took his role of husband with integrity. Here, in his home, was where he could be free to speak of his insecurities and worries with his wife.

"King David has had much victory in battle; Philistines, Moabites, Syrians and now the Edomites. His chariots have brought back many spoils from other lands. You should have seen the golden shields we just acquired! King David offered one to me for my faithful service, but I thought it best to keep it in the palace armory."

"I bet that is a fine piece of weaponry to see!"

Uriah smirked. "Have Anna show you. Benaiah took his golden shield home." Bathsheba laughed with her husband. "I'll do that on our next bread baking day."

The silence between them was brief, but Bathsheba could tell that something was troubling him. She patiently waited as he weighed his words and shook his head.

"I fear that our victories are actually helping our formidable enemies to rise against us."

"What do you mean?"

"With the victory at Moab, there is now nothing stopping the Assyrian army from attacking the garrisons here in Jerusalem."

"The Lord has given King David victory wherever he goes."

"Yes, amid all the battles, the king has been seeking anyone from the house of Saul so that he may show kindness to the family for the sake of his best friend, Johnathan. Yet, I fear he is distracted with this personal goal while a bit unaware of the impact that the death of Nahash, King of the Ammonities may have."

"Oh? Isn't that the king that King Saul defeated?"

"Yes, my wife. I am always pleased with how versed you are with political events of our nation. Nahash later conquered the tribal lands of Reuben and Gad, larger portions of the land we recently won back from the Moabites, but the Ammonities may keep the grudge and seek revenge under a new king."

Bathsheba nodded and worried over the frown that furrowed on Uriah's brow as he continued. "Most recently, King David sent word to Hanun, son of Nahash, condolences for his father's death. He wanted to deal fairly with him, since Nahash dealt fairly with Saul, and this would satisfy the king's soul in wanting to honor Johnathan. Word from our messengers have told us that Hanun misinterpreted the condolences and saw it rather as an act of aggression and political espionage. He shamed David's servants by tearing their tunics and sending them home half shaved."

"Good gracious! What did the king say?" Bathsheba was shocked at such arrogance. Uriah was about to answer when there was a knock at the door. Benaiah greeted the couple warmly, but clearly had an important message to deliver. Bathsheba got him a cup of wine while the two men sat near the fire.

"The Ammonites know they have provoked the gracious nature of King David and have sought the Syrians near Damascus to aid them in their defense. Joab has returned home to report that the Ammonites and the Syrians have retreated for now, but the king has called for all warriors to be on alert. We could be called back to the battlefield sooner than expected."

Bathsheba's heart fell as she saw the realization cross her husband's face at Benaiah's words. Battle again. Months alone without Uriah by her side. Worried sick that he would be wounded or killed was a reality every military wife faced on a regular basis. They had just began to speak about starting a family. This would now have to wait. Seven months had already gone by which were usually longer than most couples waited to have a baby. Why hadn't God opened her womb? Her arms ached to hold Uriah's child. A baby would comfort her in the long hours while he was away at war. Bathsheba looked down at the table of dishes. The bowl of soup became blurry as her eyes filled with tears.

"Surely the Syrians will come to their senses and not side with the Ammonites against Israel!" Uriah exclaimed. His friend only shrugged and accepted Bathsheba's offer for soup. The men sat late into the night speaking of packing up once more for the battlefield and Bathsheba went to bed alone, already lonely for Uriah as she knew she would be for many nights to come. She began rehearsing the answers she would give the women as they asked again why she was not yet with child. Her frustrated tears wet the pillow.

CHAPTER THREE

As the morning dew continued to rise off the flowering bushes outside her front door, she watched as the horses disappeared on the horizon from outside her home in the city wall. Anna and Bathsheba stood holding each other, fresh tears wetting their cheeks. Their group of houses were full of the gathering women whispering comfort to each other listening to the battalion of their husbands in their clanging armor grew faint as the men left the comforts of home to do battle for their king and country.

"May Jehovah God keep them safe during battle." Anna whispered. With a parental squeeze, she smiled and tried to put up a good front. "Come. Let me show you that recipe for poppyseed bread that I told you about." Bathsheba tried to smile back, but her stomach churned and she worried for her husband's safety. She was sad that she had yet to produce a child from their union; it would have filled the hours while he was away. It would have saved her from the sympathetic smiles of the women who assumed her barren womb was a judgement from Jehovah. She wanted to tell them about the virginity cloth from her marriage bed. She had done nothing wrong. For now, Bathsheba assisted Anna with her children. She especially liked to cradle little Daniel as he drifted off to sleep and longed for the day when her arms would be filled with a child belonging to Uriah. She sent another silent prayer up to Jehovah for such a gift. Please God, please, please . . . please . . . please. She repeated the plea until her throat ran dry and she swallowed hard.

The weeks passed. Bathsheba caught herself scanning the horizon daily. Listening for the sounds of hoofbeats and the return of Uriah. She would pass the civil courts in the city gates and try to listen for any word of how the battle was faring. Anna's children could be counted on for laughter and such delight that made her heart happy during such times of loneliness. As she rocked Daniel to sleep one afternoon, she watched Micah who was a boy no more than two, fascinated with a locust that had been crawling on a reed near the stream. He giggled as it crawled across his palm. Anna shook her head, watching the same scene nearby.

"Perhaps that one will be a shepherd, he enjoys the outdoors so."

"You and Benaiah have been greatly blessed by the Lord with such children."

Anna touched her arm, reading between the lines. "Your time will come, Bathsheba. God will bless your womb as well."

"My husband must be home long enough." Bathsheba tried to joke, but the pang in her heart made her voice break a bit. Anna smiled, acknowledging the effort and agreed. "The wife of an officer is not easy. Perhaps if we were married to a tax collector, or from the tribe of Levi, or even a shepherd, at least they would be home."

"A shepherd?" Bathsheba crinkled her nose. "They would not smell as good when they returned from a day in the fields." Anna laughed.

"Did you know, I heard that King David was once a shepherd as a boy." Bathsheba tried to imagine it as Anna continued.

"He rose in fame among his older, stronger brothers when he slain the Philistine giant with a shepherd's sling!"

"Yes, I have heard this tale as well. Uriah told me about it as he was charting King David's history with the prophet Nathan one day. I suppose to David, Goliath was nothing more fierce than a wild lion, something he had encountered while tending the flocks as a boy."

Anna shook her head. "Don't kid yourself. It must have been terrifying facing a man that stood as tall as the pillars of our house! I heard Goliath rose a full two heads above most men. Why, he'd have to duck to come inside for dinner."

Bathsheba giggled nervously. "Like you would have such a guest at your table!"

Anna snorted. Bathsheba's heart swelled with pride as her recalled moments of Uriah's bravery. "Uriah also told me of a time when he was a boy when he calmed a spooked donkey from teetering off a precipice. I would have been terrified of falling!"

Anna giggled. "Listen to you dreaming of your man! Yes, I heard that David is like Beneniah and Uriah. He is man who feared Jehovah God and trusted in His strength to help him bring Goliath down." Anna nodded. "Yes, I believe his faith in God is what has made our king so successful in battle with other nations. And, that faith is what will make our husband's feet swift in returning home from this one as well." The woman sat in silence for a moment, watching the children splash in the stream. Jehovah would watch over their husbands. Uriah was one of the Mighty Men, David's closest circle. Surely God would make sure that he would return unharmed. Bathsheba was sure of it.

It was a week later when Bathsheba received a letter from her husband on the battlefield. She had been so excited to receive word from her husband, she forgot to give the messenger cakes that she had just baked. She opened the scroll with trembling hands and smiled at the recognition of his handwriting.

"My dearest wife,
battle always brings a mix of emotions to me.
I am motivated to honor our nation and serve under such a mighty man as King David. Sometimes I feel as though we are a motley crew of rugged debtors, and being a Hittite foreigner, I am awed that I have been given such an honorable position in such a reputable band of soldiers. Jehovah has proved Himself to be so faithful to us, my love. We are north of Heshbon, staked out in a cave we discovered here for protection. The howling wolves and bitter cold nights make me homesick for your warm embrace and delicious stew.
Joab is a good commander. I trust him. Like David, he is a man who trusts God and mobilizes us onward, confidant in our victory over these Ammonites.
I will return to you soon, my love.
I look forward to the day when I can be with you for longer than just a few weeks. Perhaps by next spring, we will have a child we can bring to the temple for dedication by the priest. Until Jehovah brings me home to you, continue to pray for our safety and for our spirits. They are uplifted knowing we are here on the battlefield for our country's honor.
All my love, Uriah"

Bathsheba re-rolled the scroll and held it to her chest. How she missed Uriah. She went to a tunic he had left in their home and smelled it, repeating the words of her husband that she just read. Pray for our safety and for our spirits.' I do, my love.' She whispered. 'Please hurry home.'

Her cycle ended a few days later. With each passing *niddah*, it reminded her that she and Uriah had yet to have a child of their own, once more wondering how many cycles would pass until her womb was occupied with a child. She called for her attendants who prepared her bath for her one evening. She tarried in her bedchamber, wishing Uriah was there sleeping. She heard her sister Sarah call that the bath was ready and she went to the roof to be washed as the Torah instructed women to do. The chatter among the women was normal and Bathsheba was cheered with the talk of women.

Suddenly, it got quiet. The only sound was water falling off her shoulders as she stood waist deep in the water. Her attendants continued to sponge her but the talking had ceased. It reminded Bathsheba of birds when a jackal was prowling nearby. Somehow they knew danger lurked and would grow silent in their apprehension. Her skin reacted to the change in the room as well, prickling as if the water had grown cold and her eyes began to scan to see what was different. What caused her maidens to grow quiet? What was nearby? Her attendants had dropped their heads so their eyes would not make contact with hers as she continued to look about. The setting sun caused a glint of something shiny there on a nearby balcony. It was evening, no one should be here but bathers. All would be inside preparing for meal but something shone as the sunlight reflected on it. Bathsheba squinted a bit and realized it was the glint of a crown. The bright flash ceased revealing a sapphire and ruby encased in the circle that framed King David's head. He was staring at her. Unashamed and penetrating were his eyes. She turned to the right so that her exposed breasts were no longer in his view. How long had he been standing there?

She felt a flush rise to her cheeks and quickly checked to see if her maidens noticed, but their eyes were still downcast into the water.

"Bring me a towel." She whispered to Miriam who was standing to her left. She arose from the water with a slushing noise that seemed to return all other murmur to the bathing chamber. The attendants started chatting again, although in softer tones, Bathsheba noticed. She tried to wrap the towel around herself self consciously as she stepped out of the water quickly. She slipped a bit on one of the rocks and Sarah caught her elbow.

"Thank you." Bathsheba murmured and the two women looked at each other. So much was in Sarah's eyes. Bathsheba saw fear and confusion. Perhaps she felt she would be punished for not notifying her that a man was nearby and the bath would perhaps need to wait. Maybe like herself Sarah was fearful that it was the king who had seen her naked. He had the power to stone such indecency. She shook like a leaf as she dressed in her tunic. What was he doing there? Wasn't he supposed to be with his troops on the battlefield? Why had he stayed behind?

The kind words she had just read from her husband's letter to her now twisted in fear as she wondered what Uriah would think if word got back that their king had seen his wife's nakedness. Her mouth went dry and she covered her head dropping to her knees near her bed. Oh, Adoni, please regard your humble maidservant. I was cleansing after my *niddah* and did not intentionally provoke the eye of a man who is not my husband. Please be a gracious God.

The food at dinner that night and was tasteless and dry. Bathsheba was afraid to swallow because of the lump in her throat. She could not shake the doom she felt at the king's stare. When she closed her eyes, she could still see the squint of his brow focused on her like a predator closing in on prey. She desperately kept calling out silently to God for peace and direction. There was a knock at the door that startled her head to snap up from her prayer. Who would be calling at this time of night? She heard Sarah open the door and commotion in the front room. She came out from her bedchamber to see a page from the king's palace standing there. Her stomach began to churn more ferociously and she licked her lips nervously.

"Bathsheba, daughter of Eliam, wife of Uriah, the Hittite?"

Bathsheba nodded silently and scanned the eyes of Sarah and Miriam standing nearby. Once again, their eyes were downcast to the floor and she could gain no morsel of support from them. "Come with me!" the page demanded. Bathsheba quickly shoved her feet into the sandals sitting by the door and followed the man out. The door slammed so fiercely behind her, she jumped. It signified that she was without protection here on the hall summoned by the king's court. Her first thought was one of dread. Something had happened to Uriah on the battlefield. Then she remembered her bath a few hours ago and shivered anew. She was then convinced that she was being punished for her nakedness. King David was angry with the behavior of one of his soldier's wives and she was going to be dealt with severely. She tried desperately to swallow the sobs that were threatening to undo her.

They came to an opening, flanked with two sentinels on either side. The page opened the door for her and stood by, indicating she was to walk in. She bowed her head in submission as she passed the two men at the door. As soon as she crossed the threshold, the page shut the door behind her. Not only did she feel vulnerable like she did in the hall, but now she felt trapped. Be with me, Adonai! She silently panicked as she looked about the room. A few torches burned on the walls, revealing an ornate canopied bed. From the shadows in a corner, a figure moved toward her. She forced her head down in submission once more, her heart pounding so hard Bathsheba was sure it would come right out of her chest.

"Bathsheba." She heard her name from the man that now stood before her. She dared to look up and realized she was looking into the eyes of King David himself. He offered a hand to her. He had a large ring on one hairy finger. A large ruby surrounded in gold that matched the stone she had seen glinting on his crown.

"Yes, my lord."

"Come, sit. May I offer you some figs or grapes?" He motioned to a platter that sat next to the bed. She shook her head and sank onto the softness at the edge of the bed. Keeping his eyes on her, she watched as he went to the platter and slurped up a few grapes himself. She sat there silently, her mind paralyzed with fright as to what her fate might be.

"You are a very beautiful woman." He murmured haltingly. Her hands ran cold and the prickled skin began to crawl around her neck. "Did you know I play the lyre? Would you like to hear a song? I have written many Psalms." He pointed to a musical instrument sitting on an armed chair by the window. She allowed her eyes to take it in, but did not answer him. A song? Was this customary before issuing a decree of punishment? Her eyes brimmed with tears. Seeing this, he put the grapes down on the platter and sat beside her on the bed.

"Shhhh. Calm yourself. I did not call you here for trouble."

"My lord?" she asked, still looking in her lap, not daring to raise her eyes in the presence of the king. His hand began stroking her hair. Instinctively, she tensed.

"Shhhh." He said again, as if he was trying to lull a child to sleep. "There is no need for fear. I'm not going to hurt you."

His hands brushed her shoulder. The coldness of her hands shot to her neck where his fingers were entangled in her hair at her nape. "You are so beautiful." His hands made her head lean in to touch his. He breathed in deeply to smell her hair and grunted in satisfaction. He began to kiss her forehead and the sickening realization hit Bathsheba. The king meant to rape her! He knew who she was, for the page had summoned her by name. He knew her husband was Uriah, for the page had stated that as well. Her mind raced. This man whom Uriah spoke of often was a man who feared the Lord. Who Jehovah had given countless victories to and prospered the land of Israel under his leadership. King David was revered and honored among his people. Yet here she was, in his bedchamber, being taken like a lamb. She dared not argue or fight. Women could be executed for merely speaking out of turn with the king.

She was transported to her wedding night. When this act was foreign and curious and yet when her heart was with Uriah it felt right. Like Yahweh had intended for a husband and wife to share. She remembered the virginity cloth and the honor it brought Uriah and her father that they had followed God's law of betrothal and waited. She had been a maid at their wedding and Uriah was the only man she had ever been with. But tonight, that would all change. She would forever be unclean, unrighteous, an immoral woman in the sight of God. Her mind silently screamed to Him, where are you Adonai? I am frightened! Why are you allowing this to happen to me?

David's chest was harrier than Uriah's and he tore her tunic off hungrily, not at all with the same gentleness Uriah expressed to her when they would come together. The little cries she released in surprise seemed to spurn David on in his desire as he took her with all the force of a warrior confronting a garrison. The pain she was experiencing in her heart was as piercing as the burning she physically felt in her violated body. All sound seemed to still and the torture continued for what felt like an eternity. Bathsheba tried to think of herself as far away from the palace as she could but David's hands dug into the skin on her shoulders.

She dressed quickly when it was over and didn't turn to look at him when she was instructed to leave the room. The same page was waiting for her outside the door to escort her back to the unfriendly hallways to her own home. The home she shared with Uriah. As soon as she was alone in her own bedchamber, she wept bitterly. She felt so violated, so betrayed. But worst of all, she felt alone. Forsaken by her God and separated from her husband. She knew things would never be the same again.

CHAPTER FOUR

Bathsheba was able to keep her secret of her night with the king. Anna didn't suspect a thing, and she hadn't heard from anyone official from the king's circle in over a month. If her maidens suspected anything, mercifully, they said nothing. Bathsheba searched their eyes, but they never betrayed any judgement. Since her wedding to Uriah, the stain of her monthly cycle had been a painful reminder of the baby she still did not have. But the day came when her *niddah* was due and it didn't come she began to feel a flutter of panic. Perhaps if was her stress that caused it to delay. When she couldn't keep her porridge down the next morning, she knew. What should have been exciting news, was the most terrifying. With Uriah still away at battle, Bathsheba knew there was only one man who could take credit for fathering this child. She spent two days fasting and praying, trying to decide what to do. She called for Miriam, her sister.

"Please send word that I need audience with the king."

Miriam's face distorted into shock. "What? No one asks to see the king! Certainly not a woman."

Bathsheba shook her head insistently. "I just need to get a message to him. If I write one out, could you deliver it to the king's steward?" Frightened by the look on her sister's face, she hesitantly agreed to deliver her message and she received confirmation that the message was delivered. David was strangely silent. He sent no response. She wasn't exactly sure what she expected from the king. A word of wisdom? An apology perhaps? She continued to exist in her loneliness and prayed intently to Yahweh for direction. Anna began to notice her friend's distance and asked many times what the problem was, but Bathsheba could never voice the atrocity done to her at the palace. She went through the motions of every day life as the wife of an officer in the king's army away at battle; a prestigious position, but her dark secret was growing in her womb. It began to get difficult for her to conceal her pregnancy and decided to finally tell Anna. She invited her over one afternoon.

When Anna arrived, she was breathless with news of her own. Distracted by her own message, she didn't notice Bathsheba's growing belly but sat down with her at the table and took her friend's hands in her own.

"I hear that Uriah is home." Anna said to her excitedly.

"Who told you this?" Bathsheba asked incredulously.

"Benaiah sent word to me through courier. His scroll said that King David was seeking to honor Uriah for his faithful service with a leave. Uriah has been seen at the king's chambers for the past two days."

Bathsheba's heart leapt at the news. Could it be true? She was flooded with hope. Uriah would understand. Her love would know what do after these long months of feeling so alone. She made arrangements to be part of a group of women who brought food to those who had been wounded on the battlefield. As she was sharing cakes with some of the men, she searched for Uriah. A few times, she was courageous enough to ask some men but none had seen him. Then she spied him in a corridor next to the room where she was serving food. Their eyes met and she was sure she noticed the excited charge in his eyes at seeing his wife. They exchanged a smile. Then with a pained expression, he was engaged in a conversation with another soldier and walked with him up the corridor away from her. She followed them until they were out of sight. Her heart sank. Perhaps he would come home tonight. She would just have to be patient a little while longer. She continued to pass out her cakes to the men and prayed a prayer of thanksgiving to Adonai who had brought her husband home healthy, not among the wounded here. She inadvertently stroked her belly and wondered how God was going to work this situation out.

There was a knock at her door that evening. She stumbled on a stool and overturned a bowl of figs trying to get to the door. It was Uriah at last! She couldn't wait to hold him in her arms after months of separation. She tore open the door and found a soldier in his uniform standing at her door. He nodded to her as was customary in greeting the wife of an officer who ranked higher than himself.

"Are you Bathsheba, wife of Uriah the Hittite?"

"I am." Bathsheba nodded, still surprised that Uriah was classified by his origin of birth. "I have a message for you from your husband." He handed her a scroll, gave another official nod then pivoted to leave. She thanked him and closed the door. Gathering her tunic, she sat at the table for a moment just staring at the message, afraid to open it. What if the king had told him the secret? Was her husband rejecting her by not coming home? Was he ashamed of her and making arrangements to put her away as the law decreed for adultery? How she wanted to explain to him personally. What was she to do? She couldn't deny the king! That in and of itself was a death sentence! Trembling, she unrolled the scroll and smiled at the handwriting that brought her such comfort.

"My darling wife,
How I have missed you these long months on the battlefield. What an honor to be given a leave of absence during the fighting.
I was able to give King David a full report of the happenings at the front line and how Commander Joab was doing. I am so thankful to be put in his charge.
My king instructed me to go home and wash my feet, quite a holiday from the awful realities of war. Part of me wanted nothing more than to go home and be your husband, not a warrior. As I left the king's presence, I was given a banquet of food to dine from and I wanted to share it with you. When I saw you this afternoon, I wanted to take you in my arms as I have longed to do. I have missed the softness of your touch, your encouraging words and outpouring of love.
It cheered me much to see you serving the wounded men, brave soldiers they were and then I realized my responsibility. Please forgive me, wife, for I am not able to come see you this visit. It would not be honorable. The ark of Israel and Judah are living in the tents, Joab and all the other men I serve with are still encamped in the open fields north of here near Rabbath, a great distance away.
How could I go home and enjoy your pleasures, dear wife? I have a passion for the things of God even though I was born a Hittite and am not a native Jew, I serve in His army alongside my countrymen.
I have decided to sleep at the threshold of my king. He is sending me back to the battlefield tomorrow with a message for my commander, Joab.
It will be an honor to be a courier for my king. Please understand and forgive my decision. I pray that God speed the battle so that the months will be short until I can

return home to your arms for good and start the family that we have dreamed about.
With all my love, Uriah."

Bathsheba was sobbing now, large racking spasms that sent her gasping for breath as she travailed and wailed into the evening. She would not see Uriah. Her husband had more integrity than her king! David had charged Uriah to come home to her so that the child could be passed off legitimately as Uriah's. He was trying to cover his sin! Her husband's impeccable work ethic foiled the plan. There would be no reunion between husband and wife. Not yet, not tonight. Bathsheba slid off the stool onto her knees as she continued to wail. She slumped her face forward on the ground, pleading with Jehovah to provide another path out of this desert of loneliness. She was sure she would not be able to bear it one more day. What would Uriah say now when he returned home and she was with child knowing he had not lain with her? What would become of her?

The hours seemed to pass slowly, the night was so still. A cricket would chirp every now and then, but it seemed like the world was grieving for her. She continued to scan the horizon for days after that, searching for the return of her Uriah for good. She still had not received any official word from the royal court regarding her pregnancy. Weeks turned into another month. It was far beyond the time when she could no longer hide the reality. She let her neighbors think it was Uriah's. He had been home on leave recently, hadn't he? It was easier than facing accusations or questions. She knew she would have to face the truth when Uriah returned. But for now, those around her could be happy that Adonai had finally blessed them with a child. Anna had begun fashioning a blanket for their little one, and Bathsheba found the guilt of not telling her friend the truth was a heavy yoke to bear.

"How are you feeling?" Anna asked her as the women walked to the well with their empty jugs, a few days later.

"I miss my husband." Bathsheba confessed. She missed him more than she realized.

Anna nodded absently. "Yes, it is hard to be without your husband when they are serving at war. Fear not, by friend. There are many good midwives in town. Even if Uriah does not make it home before the birth, you will be cared for. I told you Adonai would open your womb. What a blessing He has provided you in your faithful patience!"

"Bathsheba!" A shriek erupted as the women looked up from the well to see Miriam running toward them. Her face was stained with tears and she grabbed Bathsheba in a hug with such uncharacteristic force that Bathsheba's heart leapt into her throat. Anna found her voice first.

"Miriam! Calm yourself. Whatever is the matter?"

"News, such terrible, terrible news from the battle!"

Bathsheba could read it on her face but would not accept it. She gathered her tunic and ran away, leaving her water jug, Anna and Miriam at the well behind her. She heard them calling after her, but she ran. She kept running, like she was a young girl until she had reached her house when the tears were threatening to spill out over her cheeks. She stopped short and gasped for breath as two soldiers were standing outside her front door.

"Bathsheba? Wife of Uriah, the Hittite?" they asked politely.

"No, no, no, no….." Bathsheba began to wail and her strength left her legs. She was sinking to her knees in sobs when Anna and Miriam caught up with her, and flanked themselves on either side of her for support. They each grabbed one of her arms and spoke for her to the soldiers.

"Sir, do you have a message for the wife of Uriah?" Anna asked, her voice breaking mid sentence.

The soldier on the right nodded to the other and began to speak in an official tone. "I am sorry to report that your husband Uriah was killed this morning in the line of duty."

"Noooooooooooo!" Bathsheba's wail echoed off the walls of the houses. She no longer cared what people thought of her, she had carried this burden alone while her husband was away. Now, God saw fit to allow him to be killed in battle as well. Uriah was never coming home. She was a warrior's widow. Anna and Miriam joined Bathsheba in her mourning wails. She fell to the dusty ground, put her face down in the dirt and grabbed handfuls of dust in her palms. She beat the ground with such angry force and tasted the dust on her parched lips as she continued to travail. The commotion began to bring people out of their homes to witness the spectacle and the murmur of the tragic news spread like wildfire. Uriah has been slain in battle. Bathsheba's husband is dead. The soldiers that had delivered the message slipped away quietly in the crowd that was growing louder in customary responsive mourning and lamentation.

Bathsheba closed her eyes tight and raised her head to the sky. She let a piercing howl escape from her lips. Where was God? Had she not been faithful to her husband Uriah? Had Uriah not proven to be a righteous warrior? Did God not see how King David had raped her and she now silently was carrying his bastard child within her? Then her husband had been home and she had been denied his touch. But now, God allowed him to be killed? What was to become of her? She screamed until her voice grew horse and felt the weight of Anna fall on her in a vain attempt to comfort her friend. Bathsheba didn't think there was any chance of recovering from this. This grief, the shame and injustice was going to kill her; slowly strangle her from within. Her fingers tore at her throat as if her air supply was being cut off. There is no light in a pit as dark as this.

The week of the shadow of death lingering at Uriah's home had begun.

CHAPTER FIVE

The days passed and the mourning continued. Bathsheba welcomed the mood for it seemed the world had finally fallen in step with where her heart was all these months alone. Anna and Benaiah had her stay in their home and accepted the meals people would bring with their condolences. Bathsheba wore sackcloth with no jewelry as a sign of her mourning. When the mourners had left one evening, the three sat near the fire and were sharing memories of Uriah.

"What a man of integrity he was." Benaiah commented. "It was an honor to serve alongside him, for he challenged me to be the best husband and soldier I could be. When he was on leave that last time before this tragedy, he returned to the battle heavier than when he had left. I asked him about it, assuming that a leave home would cheer spirits, not leave one so melancholy." Benaiah poked at the fire with a stick as he recalled the memory. Bathsheba listened with Anna, wiping silent tears from her cheeks as they fell.

"If it had been me that was granted leave, I would have been home with Anna my wife. you wouldn't of had to ask me twice. But not honorable Uriah. He told me on his return that it pained him not to see you, Bathsheba. He missed you so. But he could not enjoy his visit knowing that he had left us in the fields. Even when the king offered him much drink, Uriah was upset that he allowed himself to be intoxicated and it seems to steel his resolve even more to be a man of integrity. He never left the kings door the entire visit. I understand he even slept there on a mat instead of in the barracks with the others home on leave."

"He would have been a good father." Anna mused softly. Bathsheba stroked the child in her belly that had begun to move as it grew. Anna's face frowned in realization as she faced her. "Uriah never came to see you on this leave?" Bathsheba stared back at her, terror rising in her throat. Anna's eyes dropped to Bathsheba's belly and her mouth hung open. Bathsheba silently shook her head, willing her friend to stop accusing her as Benaiah continued his reverie.

"I couldn't understand it. Uriah had returned with a message for our commander, Joab. His face was crestfallen, as though they told him of a great loss, the message was not a good one. Jolly Joab was not himself that night and he sent Uriah into the heat of the battle the next morning. At the very front, can you imagine? Uriah ranked much higher than the enlisted men that were out in that position, but Joab quietly said he was just following orders."

"He was placed at the frontlines?" Anna asked incredulously and Bathsheba looked at Benaiah. Could this be true? The terror from within her began to grow.

"It was no surprise that he met his demise there. The fighting was so fierce, the Ammonites have many great archers. Joab sent word back to King David of how Uriah had fallen, quoting a battle scene that happened during the time of the judges. The fighting had got too close to the city walls, which to a commander like Joab with much military strategy knowledge would have seen such a move as folly, for more friendly fire can happen there close to the panic of city inhabitants." Benaiah looked up as if reading from the recesses if his mind.

" 'Who killed Abimelech, the son of Jerubbesheth? Did not a woman throw a millstone from a window and strike his head? Uriah, your servant is dead as well.' King David responded with a flippant 'the sword devours one as well as another.' He might as well have said 'these things happen.' I expected more grief from the king on Uriah's behalf, he was so beloved by all the Mighty Men."

Puzzled, Bathsheba listened to the tale. Knowing the truth, it sickened her to follow the logic of events. While her husband was away, she was called to the king's bedchamber to satisfy his thirst of lust. Then, when she discovered she was with child and sent word to the king, he brought her husband home to cover up the conception. Her husband would not come home to her out of moral obligation as a soldier, so now he was killed in battle? Seemed so convenient, it tidied up all the details.

Anna vacillated between her husband and her friend. Both wore pained expressions but the truth still seemed to elude her. "What are you thinking, Benaiah?"

"I am afraid! I trusted King David. I fight for his kingdom on a regular basis and Uriah was one of the best Might Men I knew. Why David would put him in such a vulnerable position makes me question my own safety! Am I just a body to the king that he may use me with such abandon? Will I be the next to take a sword?"

"And you." Anna turned to her friend. "How are you feeling?" Bathsheba looked at her but no words would come. She swallowed hard and licked her lips.

"Like Benaiah, I do not trust the king. His choices have cost me my husband, my future and my happiness. Grief will follow me all the days of my life and I will be a forgotten widow left to beg at the city gates in a city which is not my home."

"But, your child . . ." Anna began to say then stopped herself. It sounded accusatory to Bathsheba. Her furious stare silenced anymore idle talk on the matter. Bathsheba checked the days in her head. She only had three more mourning days left, and only a month left before her child was due to be born. What would become of her?

Anna sensed her exhaustion, helped her to bed that night, giving maternal encouragement of hope that lay beyond the days of mourning. To her great relief, Anna didn't mention her suspicion surrounding her pregnancy. Instead Anna assured her that Jehovah would bring happiness back to her heart and that if she would just wait on Him, she would see how He would work it all out. Bathsheba hoped so.

A few days later, she was packing up the last of her household items. Having finally heard from the palace, she was asked to report to his majesty's side, for he would take her as his wife and give legitimacy to what everyone assumed was Uriah's child. The town raved about the tenderness of King David's heart to care so for the widow of one of his fallen soldiers. Like the night when the whole nightmare had begun, how could she deny the king? She remembered packing up her wedding trousseau and traveling here to Jerusalem with Uriah after they were married so he could resume his position in the royal military. She had been sad to leave her family but excited at the bright future that lay ahead of them.

Now, as she packed up her belongings, it felt as though she was packing all the hopes and dreams of those days away for good. None of it would come to fruition, her life had taken such an unexpected turn. Hopeless, she wondered what living in the palace would be like. She would be living as a queen, her offspring in line for the throne! Bathsheba silently prayed that Adonai would go with her and cheer her spirits as she walked into her new world. As for her, she no longer cared what life brought. She had resigned herself to a pitiful existence, forever marred by the cruelty of those in power. As she walked passed the officer's quarters, she saw Anna kneading bread. As the two women's eyes met, Bathsheba knew that her dear friend knew the truth about why she was moving to the palace and whose child grew inside her. It caused fresh tears to well up and to her eternal gratitude, she saw a tear fall down Anna's face as well. It was not easy being a soldier's wife. It was impossible to be a woman subject to a king.

She was brought to the palace and shown the wing of Queens where the wives of King David already resided. She passed one of the chambers and caught the condescending glance of a woman who dripped with royalty. In an instant, she had sized Bathsheba up with a glance and dismissed her as insignificant. Bathsheba didn't know who she was, but felt very unwelcome. She was given a furnished room of her own and left to unpack with the held of three handmaidens. Bathsheba missed the council of her old friends, but knew like her old life she must put them out of her mind.

"My lady." One of the handmaidens greeted her with a low, respectful bow.

Bathsheba had her stand. She was a teenager and quite pretty. "What is your name, child?"

"Rachel."

"Ah, after Jacob's favored wife?"

"Yes, ma'am. Can I assist you in unpacking?"

"Certainly." Bathsheba sat on her new bed. She looked around the ornate fixtures and wondered if she'd ever get used to such luxury. She stubbornly resolved to not enjoy this life but was relieved to see she would never go hungry. "Can you tell me of King David's wife, the Queen? I heard she was a daughter of King Saul."

"Yes ma'am. Michal helped hide the young king from King Saul when he sought his life. She sided with her brother Jonathan and conspired against their father to save David's life. There was a story of how she helped lower him out the city walls from a window . . .I understand she loved him very much."

"Loved him? Past tense?"

"There was a time of political conflict after they were married, that her father Saul had her marry another, although David won her back. She was not happy though when David brought the Ark of the Covenant back to Jerusalem. I think she knew about the God in the Torah, but didn't approve when King David danced with joy for the Ark's return. She felt it was undignified and was quite jealous of the women of the court who were present." Bathsheba appreciated Rachel's candor. As a teen, she knew much but was without the restraint of adulthood and spoke freely. "She appears to be quite religious, even her very name 'Michal' speaks of a brook which is symbolic for water and life. Yet, she seems to be more fond of rules and legalities than of worship. The Lord has seen fit to close her womb, perhaps in judgement, for she has no children. Since the king has forced her to return her, she looks like she has just sucked on a bunch of bitter herbs. I don't think she likes it here much." Rachel seemed smug as she folded some of Bathsheba's garments for her. Bathsheba remembered the woman who had looked at her so sternly moments ago and assumed that was probably Queen Michal.

"You speak out of turn." Bathsheba gently reminded her to which Rachel nodded but didn't seem bothered by. Perhaps she didn't view her as a true Queen, but an outsider and her insecurities overwhelmed her once again.

"There are others." Rachel dangled a carrot that caught Bathsheba's curiosity.

"Oh?"

"There is Achino'am, which means 'brother's delight.' She and the king can been seen walking together and talking. They talk and talk and talk." Rachel rolled her eyes dramatically.

"Then there's Abigail. I like her a lot. She was married to a horrible man with a distasteful reputation but she is a woman who speaks her mind and this integrity caught King David's eye. There was an incident when Abigail's husband would not pay a debt he owed the king and had earned a place of execution. Abigail gave the king three donkeys loaded with food to give to the king as pardon for her husband, even though the whole town knew he was despised. She too shares the king's love for conversation and they married when her first to ad of a husband died. She gave King David a son, Chileab. Many people find her to be quite friendly. You may too." Bathsheba was taking the information in when Rachel continued with her monologue.

"Amnon's mother is Achino'am. He's older than Chileab. Snobby Absalom's mother is Ma'acah who is the daughter of the king of Geshur. She and the king *don't* talk much." Rachel giggled. With the emphasis on lack of conversation, Bathsheba could only imagine that she was not the only woman David found pleasure in. Counting on her fingers, Rachel continued. "Then there's Chaggith who is a belly dancer and present at all of the king's parties, Abital ... whom I don't know much about and Egelah." Rachel moved closer to Bathsheba conspiringly and whispered, "Egelah means 'heifer' because she is quite a large woman." Rachel was shaking her head with a coy little smile on her face.

"That's quite a list." Bathsheba sighed. She wondered with all those women why he ever called for her all those nights ago.

"I'll say." Candid Rachel exclaimed. "There's quite a line for the throne. I hope it doesn't go to Absalom, although his head is quite large by the fact that he is the first son born by a royal marriage, since Michal didn't bear any children. Ahinoam and Abigail aren't from royal lineage. So Absalom thinks he can sweep in and someday take the throne. He is quite handsome though." She sighed.

"You have been here in at the palace for some time then?" Bathsheba asked. Rachel proudly nodded. "And my mother before me. I have aunts and sisters that are also employed in the queen's service."

"You know a great many stories." Bathsheba made it a note to guard her secrets carefully or Rachel's careless tongue would make her the topic of conversation among the servants. She surmised as a new-comer, she probably already was.

Remembering her place, Rachel snapped back into servanthood. "Is there anything else you require tonight, ma'am?"

"No thank you, Rachel. I am quite tired and think I'll retire early. It has been quite a day." Bathsheba rose and faced the young girl. "Thank you for helping me learn of the other wives here, but I must insist that you do not speak of me or my habits or my children with as much irreverence as you have shown me tonight do you understand?" She would not be the latest piece of palace gossip.

"Yes ma'am." Rachel bowed once more before leaving Bathsheba alone in her quarters. She went to the window and looked out over the houses below. She spotted the balcony where she had bathed so many months ago. She stroked her growing belly and wondered where her child would fit in the menagerie of royal women and children already clamoring for David's throne. She had been a happy wife of one man, now she was one of many wives to a man she didn't love living in a palace as a queen but she felt so alone.

Wandering outside her quarters, Bathsheba was in the royal gardens and pulled off a sprig of a fern as she listened to the stones rumble beneath her as her feet shuffled past. How would she pass her time here? How would she fit in? Everyone seemed so purposeful and moving confidently along their organized agenda. Bathsheba no longer hoped for anything in this life, so there was no motivation to do anything or to experience anything.

She had wandered to a little fountain with lily pads and frogs. She watched the ripples in the water as one dove under the surface.

"Hi."

Startled, Bathsheba turned toward the soft voice behind her. She saw a young teenager, no more than fourteen holding hands with a smaller child. Bathsheba nodded her acknowledgement.

"I'm Tamar. I am the daughter of Ma'acah, one of King David's wives. This is Chileab, Abigail's son. Another one of David's wives."

Bathsheba turned her attention back to the pond, her eyes filling with tears. Will she be introduced as 'another one of David's wives?' Nothing special. Just another stolen lamb. Sweet Tamar was not easily daunted.

"I'll leave you alone for now, but just wanted to introduce myself. I could help you get adjusted to life here. I suppose it is pretty overwhelming to you. Perhaps I'll see you at supper." Bathsheba watched her go. Tamar. The girl's name tumbled over in her head and in spite of herself, Bathsheba was relieved at the prospect of having met a new friend.

CHAPTER SIX

Bathsheba was sitting in the royal court one afternoon, accepting guests who requested audience with the king, quietly listening to the grievances and requests from David's many subjects. Abital sat next to her, holding her son, Shephatiah, Egelah was on the other side of her. Abigail sat to David's left, Chileab playing quietly at her feet. Bathsheba had settled in to the political rhythm of a royal household. The civil issues, the parties, the public opinions. They all wearied her a bit for the palace was not a restful place, but she continued to trust in God's timing and awaited the arrival of her child. The Lord's prophet Nathan entered. Bathsheba remembered him from her days with Uriah. Nathan had been documenting a historical record of all of King David's conquests that Uriah had often helped him edit. He told the king he had a parable which needed David's royal discernment on the correct way to handle the situation.

"By all means, please tell me your tale." David permitted Nathan to speak.

"There were two men, one very wealthy, and the other was quite poor." Nathan began. "The wealthy man had numerous flocks while the poor man had acquired a single young lamb. He grew quite attached to this kid and it grew with him and his children, eating scraps from the family meal at the base of their table and sleeping in his arms." Bathsheba smiled at the sweet relationship the poor man seemed to have with his young lamb. As if reading her thoughts, Nathan scanned the wives and children sitting behind the king and his gaze lingered on Bathsheba. She shivered in spite of herself.

"Now a visitor came to commune with the wealthy man and he was unwilling to part with one of his many flock to prepare a proper feast for the guest, so he took the poor man's lamb." Nathan paused for affect and it worked. David grew quite angry. He beat his fists on the arms of his throne where he sat and boomed, "How dare this wealthy man show no concern for he who had so little." Bathsheba jumped a bit at his ire and tried to fade into the background, unnoticed.

"As the Lord lives, may this wealthy man who has done this despicable thing deserves to die for his greed and he shall return the lamb to the poor man's family four times over because he took no pity on their poverty!" David decreed to Nathan with an authoritative finality. Nathan's eyes narrowed as he stared into King David's glare and with the courage that only came from the Lord. Nathan stuck his finger out and pointed at David.

"You are that man, says the Lord of Israel!" Nathan boomed with as much force as David did with his edict. Bathsheba's mouth dropped open in surprise. "God anointed you king over Israel and delivered you from Saul's wrath an what have you done? You have displeased the Lord and killed Uriah the Hittite with the sword and taken his wife as your own!" Now Nathan was pointing at her and Bathsheba felt her cheeks flush as if on fire. Was she hearing this correctly? Uriah's death was not an accident but a calculated casualty to all the sin that was unleashed that night?

"Therefore, the sword will never depart from your house because you have despised the Lord your God." Nathan prophesied. "God will raise evil against you from within your own house. For what you did in secret, God will do before all of Israel in the brightness of the noonday sun." Bathsheba was speechless. She darted her eyes from Nathan to David, not sure of what would happen next. She instinctively placed a protective arm over her womb and dared not breathe. No one said a word and the court grew silent as King David's guilt was finally exposed. Abital stopped rocking her son, and she could feel Abigail's eyes on her.

David rose from his throne and Bathsheba cowered a bit, for she was sure that he was going to strike Nathan of have him thrown in prison. His face was so distorted in a grimace. He looked about the room and licked his lips. The room grew so still; no one spoke. David took hold of his royal robe with both hands at the neck and ripped it down the front. The adornments that were sewn into the gown scattered noisily on the stone floor. David let out a guttural groan and looked up to the sky with outstretched arms.

"I have sinned against the Lord!" David cried out. Bathsheba was stunned. Uriah had held this man of God with such regard, God had blessed King David's hand and reign over and over again. Then she was ensnared into the most hopeless spiral of shame and deceit of darkness she had ever known and her world was turned upside down by this same man. She was pregnant and widowed by this schemer. Now, here he stood in front of God's prophet, confessing his sin and transparently showing his contrite heart for all the court to see. For a moment, Bathsheba felt the sweet flutter of vindication. She was the victim of this man's lust. God had seen her; heard her anguished cries and had sent word to Nathan to confront David. Now everyone would know that she was innocent! Everyone would know . . . everyone one would know! A second thought flooded into her mind. Soon word would get out to the whole kingdom.

Bathsheba's stomach churned. What would people think of her? Now living as his queen when they heard the truth? Would they think she had willingly went to the king while Uriah was still alive? But then again, perhaps this open confession was David's true character that Uriah had often praised him for. That he was a man after God's own heart. That the same faith in Adonai that he had while wielding the shepherd's sling at Goliath still resided in his heart and that with acceptance of both God's discipline and forgiveness, David would regain God's favor. Now that she was his wife in the royal household, perhaps God would see fit to bless her as well.

Pleased with what he heard, Nathan said "You will not die, David. The Lord has put away your sin. However, because of this deception of adultery with Uriah's wife and his murder, the child that is born to you shall die." A cry escaped from Bathsheba's lips. Did she hear correctly? The baby she felt moving in her womb was destined to die for his father's sin? Why must she once again pay for the sin of David? Her eyes filled with tears and her gaze met David's. She saw his humiliation and no trace of the dominating lust that had filled his face that horrible night. This gave her no comfort. Running from the room, she found solace from her handmaidens as she cried violently at the sentence. It was too much to bear. She felt as though she had lost everything and cried out to Jehovah once more. How much longer would she have to endure? How much more heartache could her soul take? How much more? How much more? She felt crushed under the immense weight of the sin and wailed up to the heavens.

A quiet knock on the door caused her handmaidens to scatter nervously. She wiped the tears from her cheeks and rose to answer the door. David stood with Nathan behind him. He cleared his throat. "My I come in?" Bathsheba's heart began to pound. He was the last person she wanted to meet at this moment, but nodded and stepped aside so they could walk into the room. She wiped the bitter, hot tears from her cheeks and tried to slow her breathing.

David reached out for her with his hand. Bathsheba scowled at it, drew her arms around her middle and turned away. David exchanged looks with Nathan. "I wanted to apologize to you, my wife." Bathsheba turned, ready to unleash her fury at him, empowered by Nathan's presence to back her up. David was down on one knee before her, head bend low. Bathsheba was speechless. Her king was humbled before her and she wasn't sure how to respond. She looked at Nathan.

"Come, let us sit for a moment." Nathan motioned to a table where Bathsheba sank into a chair, not able to trust the strength of her legs any longer. David rose and shuffled to a place across from her.

"The Lord appointed David to be king after Saul. God saw much character in him and is a man after the very heart of God." Nathan gently spoke to Bathsheba. "However, because of this great virtue he has been entrusted with, David has also found himself vulnerable to an attack from the enemy. You, my dear were caught in the middle and together, you have a difficult journey. Instead of humbling himself, David tried to hide his sin and multiplied the problem. This is why the Lord has pronounced such a devastating act of discipline by promising to take the life of your child."

Bathsheba was sobbing anew, holding her belly and rocking. David looked at her, weeping as well. "Can you ever . . . forgive me?" Bathsheba shook her head. David nodded understandingly.

"Since my coronation, I tried to lead all of Israel into trusting in the Lord our God. I wanted to bring the ark of the Covenant back to Jerusalem and have a heart to build a temple for God. He blessed me with many victories over enemies in the land, and I grown quite arrogant in my heart. I forgot that they were all blessings from Him, and thought instead that I had a mighty hand in it all. I . . . . I acted like a spoiled child." He put his head in his hands.

"I saw something I wanted and went after it at any costs. I gave no thought to you, or to . . . Uriah . . . ." saying his name, David's voice broke and he began to cry openly. It took a few moments for him to regain his composure to continue. "I am caught in a terrible net. The law commands that murder and adultery are punishable by death. I have pronounced this on others, but as king, what I am to do? Excuse myself for the same sin or throw myself upon a sword as King Saul did? I have sinned! I have been publicly humiliated! How can God use me now?"

Empowered by his unkindly outburst and the gentleness of Nathan, Bathsheba unleashed her anger on David. "I will *never* forgive you!" She hissed. "You murdered my husband! You stole my life! You sins will now cost me the life of my son! May God's judgement rain on you in torrents!"

Nathan rose and spoke authoritatively. "The Lord God is still in control. Be still." Bathsheba obediently sat back down and quieted her sobs. "Judgement will fall upon your son and his life will pay for the king's transgression." Nathan walked over to the dark corner where David was cowering. "It was right to bring Bathsheba into your house as wife. God will forgive you and bless you with another son that will be a great man of God. But you will go through a years of heartache. With the sword never leaving your household, more devastation is in store. But take heart. The Lord knows your character that the enemy tried to extinguish."

Nathan went and stood behind David, placing his hands on his shoulders like a father and walked him back to the table where Bathsheba sat. He looked into Bathsheba's eyes as he spoke, encouraging them both.

"With humility, reverence and trusting in God shall you emerge from this dark season. Be obedient to Him all the rest of your days, recognizing that all blessing comes from Him. You have been repentant and that is a powerful testimony for your people."

David looked up and locked eyes with Bathsheba. Her heart fluttered a bit. Was it possible to move past this? Was he truly repentant? She lifted a silent prayer to Jehovah, knowing that she was not in control but trusted that He was. She asked God to stay close during the next few months; they terrified her. She could not control her breathing. David reached his hand tentatively across the table. Bathsheba looked at it for a moment. Slowly, she brought her hand up from her lap so her fingers could touch his. Healing would be slow and take time. But this was a start.

CHAPTER SEVEN

Bathsheba cried out as a pang of labor hit her. She pushed with all her might. The royal midwives were by her side, giving her sips of water and massaging her back as she squatted to give birth to her child. David was outside pacing. He had not eaten anything all week, since Nathan gave his grave prophecy that the child would die. Night after night Bathsheba watched as he paced the balcony pleading with the Lord to let their son live. Now here she was, travailing in the struggle of childbirth. The child was born and let out a small cry. Bathsheba was able to hold him and spent that first precious night cradling him and singing him lullabies like she did to Anna's son Daniel all those years ago. She too was beside herself with fear as the child grew lethargic within the next few days. He stopped taking her breast and Bathsheba knew that the prophets words would come true. Within a week, the child she bore with David died.

Strangely, when David got word that the child had died and they had the royal funeral for the young heir, David seemed to snap out of his depression. Months of moody pacing, staying up at the stars and endless prayers had all come to an abrupt halt. David was resigned to the reality of the circumstance his sin had produced. Bathsheba, however, could not master the dark depression that had overtaken her. Food had no taste, the sun had lost it's brilliance and the lilacs were no longer fragrant. In recent days, she hadn't bothered to rise when the rooster called for the morning meal. David's attention turned from his son's death, to the well being of the child's mother. He went to Bathsheba's door and quietly knocked.

"Bathsheba, please open the door, I wish to speak with you." David's words were greeted with cold silence. "I know you have been melancholy and I take full responsibility for your sadness. Please open the door and hear me out."

Bathsheba quietly opened the door but refused to meet his gaze. She sat back down at the table and stared at the tiled floor.

With a raspy whisper, she asked him, "How is it that you spend night after night on your knees in the presence of God while I delivered the child and for the week that he lived, but now that he is dead you move on as if he had not existed at all? If God was going to take our son, why did I have to go through the work of labor to deliver a child I will never see grow to adulthood? Why couldn't I have died in childbirth so I wouldn't have to feel this weight of grief again. When I lost Uriah, I thought it would swallow me up. Now I fear that I will never recover."

"While our was still alive, who knew if God would intervene on my behalf with graciousness toward his servant so that the child would live. But now that he is dead, as Nathan prophecies he would due to my great sin, why now should I fast? Can it bring him back to life?"

"No! That is not fair! It was not my sin and yet I share in your punishment!" Bathsheba cried out to him. "You took my husband Uriah, you took the life I had with him while he served you with honor and now you have taken my son!" She wailed with fresh tears and beat his chest.

With tenderness she had never seen from him, David took her in his arms. "My sin was great and long reaching. I am so sorry, my wife. I am so, so sorry! Take comfort, our God is great and faithful. He will return favorably to us."

"How do you know this?" Bathsheba asked. "How can you be so sure?"

"I have seen our God working in Israel ever since I was a small child tending my father's flocks. He was there when I slay the lion and wolves that threatened the sheep. It was in His might that I depended when I accepted the taunts of Goliath and took him down to honor King Saul and save our nation. It was the Lord who saved my life from Saul's jealousy and anointed me as king. I continue to serve Him and know as difficult as the discipline was, it was just. I took my position as king and abused it in a most dreadful way. You are right, Uriah was a righteous man that I had no right to snuff out his life to hide my own guilt. I had no right to take you as my own when you belonged to him. I pray that I may someday restore your faith in me, for I love Adonai with all my heart and strive to serve him with all that I am and all that I have."

"But Nathan said the sword will never leave your house. What does that mean?" Bathsheba asked fearfully.

David shook his head and looked to the ground. "The future may hold more heartache for us, but that does not change who He is. 'He who dwells in the shelter of the Most High and abides in the shadow of the Almighty will say to the Lord, my refuge and my fortress, my God in whom I trust. Though the wicked will sprout like grass, and evildoers flourish, they are doomed to destruction forever but thou, Oh Lord, are on high forever.'"

"Our future is unseen by us, but this I know. A day in the Lord's company is better than anywhere else." David whispered. He slipped out of the room as Bathsheba's head swam. Her arms ached to hold a baby. She longed to be held by strong Uriah. She wanted to sit at the feet of her father, Eliam and have her stroke her hair like he did when she was a girl. Bile rose in Bathsheba's throat. Would God honestly ask her to live with the mad who had so much blood on his hands? And now when his sin had been found out, he was groveling and weeping like a little boy. She took a deep inhaling sob and held the breath in her chest. She closed her eyes tight and shook her head, trying to will the dark clouds of depression away lest they swallow her up for good.

She went to the window and watched the sun begin to set on the horizon. She took a few more deep breaths of air and wiped the tears from her face. She raised her chin a bit, trying to embody the royal title that had been thrust upon her. Wallowing in her sadness would do no more good than David's blubbering. Tonight, grief would have it's full measure. When the sun rose the next morning, Bathsheba decided she would also embrace the new life her at the palace on her terms. Turning from the window, she hardly believe the new resolve she had told herself. How could she possibly replace Uriah in her heart with David? Would another child ever bring comfort to the death of the son she never got to know?

"Oh Adonai, where are you?" Bathsheba whispered in her chamber. Her shaking voice seemed to be absorbed into the stone walls. Was God even listening? "I can't do this alone.

Jehovah, give me the strength I beg you. This is too great a task." She covered her face with her hands and wept bitterly. The sun continued to set and the shadows great around her. Yes, for tonight, grief would reign.

CHAPTER EIGHT

A gentle knock on the door awoke her the next morning. Rachel, one of her servants scampered into the room.

"Madam, awake! You have a visitor. It is the prophet Nathan, asking to speak with you! He is waiting in the garden."

Bathsheba rubbed sleep from her eyes. Nathan? Did she hear that right?

"Thank you, Rachel. Please tell him I will be down shortly." Bathsheba splashed some water on her face and changed into fresh clothes. She paused by the window and saw the rays of a morning sun peeking through the clouds. She remembered her vow last night. Grief had it's night. This was a new day. God's day.

She walked down to the garden and found Nathan sitting on one of the stone benches rubbing a fern in his fingers. When he spotted her, he rose and gave a respectful nod.

"Good morning, Nathan." Bathsheba greeted him. Her voice sounded too meek to her own ears but this new attitude was sheer will at this point. She would fake it until she made it.

"Bathsheba. That is a powerful name. Do you know it's meaning?"

Bathsheba nodded. "My father, Eliam told me he named me Bathsheba, daughter of the oath."

"The oath, yes." Nathan agreed. "Do you know what that means?"

Bathsheba shyly looked up and met his gaze. She saw kindness in his eyes and shook her head. Nathan turned from her and began to walk down the path between the hibiscus and aloe plants. She followed a few steps behind.

"An oath is a promise; a divine witness regarding one's future action or behavior." He stopped and turned to Bathsheba. "You *are* that witness for this future time. You will be a testimony of Jehovah's providence."

"I don't understand."

Nathan smiled and motioned for them to sit on a small retaining wall. Bathsheba's shoulders slumped and she wrung her hands in her lap. Nathan gently lifted her chin with his hands. It reminded her of her father, Eliam.

"Daughter of Promise. Providence is the protective nature of God. You are drenched in His spiritual care."

Bathsheba shook her head, disbelieving.

"I know that is difficult to grasp considering the path that led you here. You were a victim, please know that you did nothing wrong. You were a virtuous wife to Uriah and God has never forgotten you. It is unfortunate that you were caught up in David's arrogance. How he thought he could get away with his passions is despicable. That God would use me, his humble servant and prophet . . ." Nathan stopped and sighed. He looked up into the trees and Bathsheba followed his gaze. She spied a bird with a piece of yarn in it's beak, ready to weave it into a nest that was perched nearby on the branch.

"One night long ago, I was called by David of a plan he had wanted me to tell him what God revealed to me. 'Would you build a house for me to dwell in?' says the Lord. For since His hand brought Israel from Egypt, His glory has resided in a tent; a tabernacle. A place with no permanence. David wanted to be the one to build a great temple for the Lord."

Nathan looked back at Bathsheba. The kindness remained in his eyes and in his voice.

"The Lord took David when he was but a shepherd boy to be the ruler over his people, Israel. His hand has been on David ever since then, giving him victory in battle and great favor with all people. At first, I encouraged David to follow through with his great plans; what a legacy to his reign." Nathan's brow furrowed and he looked down into his lap.

"But David's heart grew proud. Independent. He rested in the favor of the Lord and got sloppy with his intentionality. Last spring, David was supposed to be at war with his men. He was caught up in what his eyes saw and made a previous mistake. That mistake grieved the Lord's heart as well. You must know that."

Bathsheba had never heard God spoken of so tenderly. His heart could break like hers? Did he feel the sadness she felt when her son died so suddenly after his birth?

Nathan continued. "God gave me a word that it would not be David who would build God a home. He will raise an offspring that will come after David and he will be the man who will build the Lord's temple and his throne will be forever. I told this to David, and he again was filled with remorse. David is a man of war and such a man will not build a house of prayer for all the nations.

"God is not done using David, but there are consequences for his sins. I spoke God's truth; the sword shall never depart from the house of David. So!" Nathan slapped his hands on his knees for emphasis. "What shall we do? What, Bathsheba will *you* do?"

"I want to leave you with this encouragement. King David is your husband now. When the prophet Samuel anointed him as the future king when Saul was reigning, the Lord called

David 'a man after my own heart for he will do everything I want him to do.' He still has many qualities that causes him to be redeemable. He was humble and quick to admitting his sin with you so publicly. He is respectful of the Almighty and trusts in His word. He is devoted to following God's leading. He may not build the temple, but he will spend the rest of his days preparing for the time when his son will."

"David needs a godly wife. A helpmate that relies on the hand of the Sovereign as he does. Bathsheba, you are that woman of virtue. David will need your wisdom and comfort in the coming days. I pray that you find it in your heart to forgive him and see what God has for you here in the palace."

Nathan stood and stretched his legs. "I have stayed too long." He bowed his head respectfully. "Thank you for listening to my words. I pray that they find their way into your heart. God is with you, daughter of the oath. Stand tall for you are free from shame."

Bathsheba watched Nathan disappear into the shadows of the portico. She looked back up into the tree and spied the bird still at work building his nest. God wants a temple. But it won't be David. David needs a helpmate. God has chosen *me*. God sees *me*. Bathsheba puzzled through the amazing love of her God. She sent up a silent prayer of thanksgiving that he would take her grief and pain like he took her shame. How her heart leapt when Nathan spoke that encouragement over her. She raised her chin and felt the title of 'queen' fit a little better than it did last night.

Smiling, she walked back into the palace. The prophet Nathan had spoke with anointing and authority and she felt a flicker of hope that Adonai would prosper she and David again after this harsh discipline. Turning back for one last look into the garden, she saw the sun had risen in the sky. was a new day.

CHAPTER NINE

In the days and weeks following her meeting with Nathan, Bathsheba made a point of seeing David not as her oppressor but as God would see him. 'A man after God's own heart.' Fallible, yes. Forgiven? Apparently. Could she do the same? She forced herself to be kind and serve him in small ways. A smile in greeting. A gently touch on his shoulder when he passed him. Picking up his sandals. Folding his garments.

A few weeks later, David sent word that he wanted to visit her chamber that night. She gave her consent. He arrived quietly and knocked. She let him in and made sure to smile. She breathed in a prayer to God to guard her heart.

"Thank you for seeing me." David said when he was inside. Bathsheba nodded. "Would you like something to drink?"

"Perhaps some water."

Bathsheba nodded again and poured him a cup. He drank it silently and avoided her eyes. He put the cup down on the table and rose. Tentatively, he reached for her hands. She allowed his to clasp them.

"I do not deserve you, but I am so grateful. How have you been since . . . since our son passed away?" He spoke the last bit in a whisper like he didn't want to ask but had to. Bathsheba gulped and licked her lips.

"I mourned for our son. But Nathan met with me awhile back and encouraged me. He helped me to see God's hand and realize that I am not alone in my sadness."

David released her hands and hung his head. Bathsheba quickly took his hands back into hers. "God has answered my prayer. I asked him to show me how he sees you. He has given me the strength that I asked for. And . . ." Bathsheba swallowed hard and her hands began to shake. She felt David's grip tighten slightly as a source of support. "I. Forgive. You." Bathsheba said with her head down. Shaking her hair back and raising her chin, she smiled and looked into David's eyes. They were pleading with her. "I forgive you." She said gently and he began sobbing. Falling to his knees, he grasped her waist. She fan her fingers through his mane of hair and bent to kiss the top of his head.

He stood and led her to a nearby couch to sit. "Thank you, Bathsheba. I have done you a great wrong and I am grateful for your forgiveness. God is so good to me."

Bathsheba nodded. "I am learning how good He has been to me too." They shared a smile. She was thankful for David's gentleness and patience with her. David turned and held his arms out to her. An invitation. She allowed herself to be brought in against his chest as he took her in his arms. She listened to him breathing as he tenderly kissed the top of her head. When they were together that night, it was different when they had first come together. Instead of being driven by selfish motives, they were joined as husband and wife, joined by the Almighty himself. It was a union reminiscent of her marriage with Uriah. Respect would be learned from these hard lessons birthed from selfish choices. Obedience to the God of their forefathers, Abraham, Isaac and Jacob would ensure that although they would live with the sword in their home, it was also said that David's kingdom would be great. What a privilege that God wove such atrocities into a sweet fabric of promise. That he would use her, Bathsheba, to play such a role in the palace of Israel. David was right. God hears us when we cry in trouble and His hand is not too short to save us. Blessed be the Name of the Lord.

CHAPTER TEN

A month passed and Bathsheba noticed once again that her *niddah* did not come when it was due time. Did she dare hope to be with child once again? When Rachel brought her fruit one morning and the pomegranate was sour in her mouth, she knew once again that God was forming new life within her womb and she rejoiced in His faithfulness to her. She was happy that the child within her was conceived from love, not from a forcible rape. She spent her days in the rhythm of life within the palace and did her best to find her place among the wives of David. She had grown very fond to Ma'acah's daughter, Tamar, a beautiful teenager that spent many hours working alongside Bathsheba in her household duties.

"How are you feeling today?" Tamar asked her as they were weaving baskets together one afternoon on in the shade of palm trees. Abigail, another one of David's wives worked silently nearby. Bathsheba stroked her belly. "I feel strong. God has opened my womb and I am hoping for a son."

"You will be a good mother, Bathsheba." Tamar looked intently at her work.

Bathsheba nudged her gently with her arm. "And Micah? How is he?" Tamar's face flushed. "How did you know?" Bathsheba softly chuckled. "I notice your long looks when we see him in the marketplace. He is a gentle boy that would make a good husband." Bathsheba noticed a troubled expression furrowing Tamar's brow.

"What is it?"

Tamar shrugged. "It is difficult being the daughter of a king. My infatuations do not concern father. Father will probably choose a husband for me from one of his political allies." Bathsheba nodded. She knew that many marriages were arranged for reasons outside of love. She recalled when she first met Uriah as a teenager. How she had watched admiringly at his strong arms when he would build with other men of their village. She had been so sure that because he was a foreigner, a Hittite, her father would never agree to allow her to become betrothed to him. But God was one of miracles, and one of the happiest days of her life was when Uriah began to look her way as well. Happier still was she when Uriah asked her father for her hand.

"Can you keep a secret?" Tamar pleaded. Bathsheba glanced over to Abigail who didn't even look up from her work, so she assumed was not listening and nodded. Secrets were horrible things to try and keep. She remembered trying to keep her first pregnancy from her dear friend Anna a few years ago. If she could help carry Tamar's burden, she was happy to try.

"I . . . I have grown afraid of Amnon."

"Ahinoam's son? What has he done?" Bathsheba knew that David's eldest son was next in line for the throne but was often shadowed by the charismatic and handsome Absalom, Tamar's brother.

"Nothing really . . . yet. I have just grown uncomfortable in his presence. I have often caught his eyes resting on me for longer than is appropriate. I am cautious when bathing. I try to keep to myself so as not to cause his eye to fall on me further." Bathsheba could certainly relate to that. She remembered how her skin crawled when he felt David's lustful gaze on her at their first meeting. She thanked God again that the relationship had since healed and grown into one of mutual respect.

"Cautious when you are bathing?" Bathsheba asked softly and watched Tamar's cheeks flush.

"I may not speak correctly, I mean . . . I know little of such things for I am yet a maiden, have not lain with any man. But I sense a different concern from Amnon for me, different that my other brothers. Even though we have separate mothers, we live in close proximity and . . . it just seems like his eye should be cast on a worthy match that would be his queen when he inherit's father's throne."

Bathsheba put a maternal hand on Tamar's knee to try and quiet her youthful nervousness. "I am glad you have trusted me with your secret. You may be a virgin, but Adonai has given us women a sense when a man yearns for them. You may be misinterpreting Amnon's actions, but it is good that you are cautious and doing what you can to protect your virtue. I will pray to God for your wisdom and peace."

"Thank you, Bathsheba. I didn't know what to do and didn't feel comfortable speaking to mother about it. She is already at odds with Ahinoam about who is quite jealous of all the attention that is given to Absalom instead of her son, Amnon."

Bathsheba chuckled. David's favorite son was already first in the hearts of the people as well. He was quite a magnificent young man and seemed more suited for reigning than Amnon who was much more awkward as Tamar spoke of. Bathsheba had noticed Ahinoam's son had more social missteps than his popular half-brother. Perhaps his attention toward Tamar was one of trying to gain acceptance from that part of the family. She made a point to notice more of the interactions between them and stand up for Tamar when needed.

"Can I ask you a question?" Bathsheba asked Tamar. She nodded. "When this child comes, I would like you to assist the midwives. You would be great comfort to me."

Tamar's troubled eyes began to dance. "Oh, Bathsheba! I would be so honored! Thank you so much for including me."

Bathsheba smiled as she watched Tamar leave and caught Abigail in her peripheral vision. She too watched Tamar leave, then met Bathsheba's gaze. Bathsheba smiled at her and she nodded. The two women had never really spoke, so Bathsheba decided to seize the opportunity and make a new friend. She gathered her baskets and moved closer to Abigail.

"Your weaving is beautiful." She complemented the work Abigail had in her lap. Abigail chuckled. "It is a talent I learned from my mother before I was married. I take pleasure in it, although being the wife of wealthy men does not require me to toil in them."

"Men?" Bathsheba approached the subject gingerly. "I understand you had a husband before you married King David." Abigail looked up from her lap for a moment and searched Bathsheba's eyes. Probably searching for truth and the absence of judgement.

"Yes, my first husband, Nabal was wealthy, but not well liked. Even his name means 'fool.'"

Bathsheba's eyes widened and she permitted herself to smile. "Why would anyone want to name their child 'fool'?"

Abigail shrugged. "We first met David when he was passing through our village with his soldiers during a battle. They approached Nabal for sustenance for the troops, but selfish Nabal refused. We had plenty, numerous herds of goats and sheep and to not be generous was like flying in the face of Jehovah." Bathsheba immediately liked Abigail's spunk in recognizing the sovereignty of God. "But I overheard Nabal tell

David's men that David was a stranger and why should we share what we have with those we don't even know. He was a fool for David's reputation as a brave and mighty warrior was known throughout the land." Abigail licked her lips and continued. "One soldier lagged behind and spoke to me when Nabal was not there. He told me that David was preparing to get revenge on such selfishness and they would soon be returning with swords. He aid it must be difficult to be married to such an ill-mannered man that would not even listen to reason."

Bathsheba nodded, remembering how she came to be David's wife. "That would be difficult to be married to a man you cannot respect."

"I quickly made two hundred loaves of bread, got some jugs of wine and gathered up five sheep from the herd, grain, raisins and some other things I can't recall and put them on donkeys to be delivered to David and his troops. I didn't tell my husband any of this for I know he would disapprove, but I feared God more. I went to speak with David after I was assured he got my provisions."

"I immediately fell to the ground and bowed in respect and asked that he would reconsider attacking my husband's house even though he had been extremely rude and selfish. I told him I knew that God was with him and that he would forgive the offense by accepting my gifts and to remember my generosity during the battle so that we too wouldn't end up as a casualty of war."

"That must have been very frightening to speak so boldly. You are a brave woman." Bathsheba commended her, again remembering her own courageous act of seeking out David to inform him that she was pregnant with his child. Abigail shrugged. "I was doing what I thought was right and for protection when my husband did not. When I returned home, Nabal was having a party and had drunk much wine. I didn't tell him what I had done until the next morning."

She paused for so long, Bathsheba touched her arm. "What happened when you told Nabal?"

Abigail shook her head. "He became very weak and ill. His heart stopped beating a week later. I have have been told by others that this was God's judgement on my husband for not being generous to David's army, but it worried me. Being a widow, even a wealthy one is not a life I wanted. But David sent for me and I gladly accepted his proposal to become one of his wives. Achino'am, mother of Amnon became his wife at the same time, so I felt a kinship with her, for we came to David's house together. I overheard you speaking with Tamar about Amnon. I can't imagine Achino'am's son behaving inappropriately like that."

"Thank you for sharing your story with me." Bathsheba smiled. It must have been nice to have a friend during her transition into David's family. God alone was with her and turned her bitter heart into one of true respect of her husband. But she was reminded to be careful. Abigail had a strong connection with Achino'am and would side with Amnon if something happened.

When Bathsheba was alone that evening in her chamber, she looked out the window at the stars that were beginning to scatter across the sky. She stroked her belly and wondered what this child would be like. Would he be strong? Would he be handsome like Absalom? Thinking of the king's sons, Amnon crossed her mind and she remembered her conversation that afternoon with Tamar. Did she have cause for concern? Surely the prince would not think to break God's holy laws of marriage. He could have any maiden in the kingdom, why had his eye landed on his sister? Bathsheba knew that sin was a destructive force to which even King David's household was not immune. But she also knew that God was gracious and forgiving and from a repentant heart can spring a well of blessing as it had with she and David. The child within her now was conceived out of a redemptive love. It wasn't too late for Amnon. Perhaps she could get a message to him to watch his step. She shook her head. She was a woman. It was dangerous enough to request audience with the king. The prince would not wish to hear a message from another one of his father's wives. Perhaps she could speak to Abigail who might be able to reason with Achino'am. She decided to let God be God and prayed an earnest prayer of deliverance. She slept fitfully that night.

A few weeks later, the time came for Bathsheba's baby to be born. The royal midwives assisted her, at at her special request, Tamar was also at her side, holding her hand. When she gave birth to a son, she named him Solomon, meaning peace. For in holding her baby in her arms, she finally found the peace of God and new purpose for her life through this child. David came to see his son a few days later.

"Are you feeling well, wife?" David asked as he gently lifted Solomon from her arms.

"Yes, thank you. I have been spoiled by my maidens who have met my every need. Solomon is a good baby, he hardly ever cries."

David smiled as he rocked his young son. He walked to the window and looked out into the morning sunlight. "For the occasion of your birth, I have written a new Psalm." He turned and looked at Bathsheba. "Would you like to hear it?"

Bathsheba smiled, watching father and son and nodded. David looked lovingly into Solomon who had begun to fall asleep in his strong arms and began to softly sing.

*"Have mercy on me, O God,
according to your unfailing love
According to your great compassion,
blot out my transgressions.
Wash away all my iniquity
and cleanse me from my sin.*

*Cleanse me and I will be clean.
Wash me and I will be whiter than snow.
Let me hear joy and gladness,
let the bones you have crushed rejoice.
Do not cast me from your presence
and take not your Holy Spirit from me.
Restore to me the joy of your salvation
and may a willing spirit be mine to sustain me.*

*I will teach transgressors your ways
so that sinners will turn back to you.
Open my lips, Lord and my mouth will declare your praise.
My sacrifice, O God, is a broken spirit and a contrite heart."*

 Bathsheba nodded again as David looked to her at the end of his song. He handed Solomon back to his mother and knelt at her bedside.
 "I do believe God has forgiven me for all I did to you, Uriah, and our first son. Solomon will stand as testimony that our Mighty God is merciful and I am but a humble servant, grateful for the chance to live according to His precepts."
 "I believe you, husband. You are not the man you were many years ago when your flesh got the best of you. This son is indeed a blessing to add to your quiver full of children and I am honored to mother such a child."

David rose and lay his hand upon her head for a moment before he nodded his head in leaving. Bathsheba looked down at her sleeping infant and prayed a prayer of her own. 'Thank you God for my healthy son. I will teach him to love you, to live with integrity and obey your commandments. Thank you for your peace that has fallen on me, your grateful servant. My heart rejoices in your restoration.'

CHAPTER ELEVEN

Absalom, in classic form, held a great banquet in honor of his newest brother, Solomon's birth. The seamstresses had woven new banners for the occasion that were hung all over the great hall in vibrant colors. The lamb was roasting on a pit outside and the air hung with the fragrance of rosemary and sage. The musicians had begun to play a lively tune on the lyres that set a tone of joyous celebration. Absalom invited a great number of subjects from the kingdom and there was much merriment. Bathsheba was seated at a table of honor with David's other wives. Only Achino'am seemed melancholy.

"What grieves you, Achino'am?" Bathsheba asked her as she ate a date from the celebration platter.

"My son Amnon is not well. He has been distracted and ill of heart for many days now."

Bathsheba protectively glanced across the table to Tamar who noticed her speaking with Ahino'am.

"I am sorry to hear so. He is not here at the celebration?"

"No, he has not been able to do much of anything. He has lain in bed groaning with such despair it worries me so. He complains of an ache in his heart, but royal doctors have not been able to find anything wrong with him."

"Is there anything that can be done?"

"He is resting at home with his cousin, Jonadab, son of David's brother. He has given a little courage to my ailing son but can give me no cause for Amnon's cloud of darkness which hangs over him day after day."

Achino'am plucked more meat off the game placed before them for the celebration.

"Amnon will be fine." Abigail pipped up, sitting nearby. Achino'am smiled at her friend as Abigail exchanged glances with Bathsheba. She remembered her conversation a few days ago with Abigail and how protective she was of Achino'am.

"I am sorry to spoil the mood." Achino'am said to Bathsheba. "Congratulations to you and your son Solomon. He looks like a healthy child."

Bathsheba smiled. "He is, God has been gracious to me." Achino'am nodded but the worried look of a concerned mother never left her face.

"The king and I used to be able to talk for hours on many subjects. He doesn't wish to hear of my concern of Amnon." Achino'am shook her head sadly.

"Cheer up, Achino'am. The king has many issues to attend to, perhaps he is particularly busy. Our household is large and takes much management. God notices your mother's heart for your son and God will heal Amnon's heart as well." Abigail patted her hand and looked again at Bathsheba.

"I have asked David to let Tamar bring Amnon some of the celebration feast tonight. He is looking so thin and needs more nutrients! He requested her presence and I pray that she will be able to cheer him more than Jonadab has been able to. She was so sweet to go." Achino'am replied.

"He requested Tamar to come?" Bathsheba asked, her own concern for Tamar rising.

"Yes, Amnon has taken a liking to her over all of David's children. She is so pretty and bakes the most delicious bread."

"Yes, but she is his half-sister. Do you think that is wise?"

Achino'am looked at Bathsheba puzzled. "What is your concern? Should his sister not bring him food to help him in his ailment?"

"Amnon should receive anything that would make him feel better from whomever can cheer him." Abigail said stubbornly.

David had come to stand behind them, clapping at the band's merry song. "Are you women enjoying yourselves? What a celebration Absalom has put on for Solomon." He laughed looking about the room. Bathsheba nodded as Achino'am grew silent and turned her gaze back to her food plate. Abigail's brow was still furrowed in the worry that was growing in Bathsheba's own heart. David moved on to greet other guest.

"What did you mean by that?" Achino'am hissed at Bathsheba. "Is my son not as worthy of his sister's baking?

Bathsheba thought quickly. "No, Tamar is a great help to me with Solomon and I would not want her to catch what ails Amnon and get the baby sick, that's all." Achino'am seemed to soften at the mother's concern for her child. Abigail did not even turn but watched the celebration. Bathsheba nodded to her as she rose from her chair, desperate to leave the conversation. She spied another one of David's wives, Chaggith lead a group of young girls in an entertaining belly dance. She had remembered when her servant Rachel had told her of Chaggith's talent with song.

She joined with her handmaidens, dancing and forgetting her concern for Tamar as she rejoiced in Solomon and God's abundance. She sang and clapped greatly enjoyed the evening. She left the banquet hall for a moment to get some air in the night sky. She went out to the balcony, still listening to the lute and lyre from the party. She sipped from her wine goblet and gazed into the star-lit sky. What a magnificent night! She could feel all the sadness of the past years melt away in this moment of hope for the future. With Solomon, Bathsheba felt as if she finally discovered her purpose and it made her happy.

She noticed Micah on the terrace, the young man that Tamar admired and went to speak with him.

"What a beautiful night!" Bathsheba said and looked up at the sky full of stars.

Micah nodded. "Absolom know how to throw a great party."

Bathsheba turned to him. "What is wrong? aren't you enjoying yourself?"

Micah smiled shyly. "You know I have grown fond of Tamar, I was hoping she would be here tonight."

"You haven't seen her?" Bathsheba asked.

He shook his head and reported that he hadn't seen Tamar all night and the familiar sense of dread began to fill Bathsheba's heart.

Suddenly, she caught movement out of the corner of her eye. She turned to see Tamar, running from the room where Amnon was said to be convalescing. She was tugging on her tunic as she ran, tears streaming down her face. Shock and horror erupted in Bathsheba's heart as she instinctively knew something was very, very wrong. She ran back into the banquet hall and quickly scanned the room. She found Abigail and Achino'am huddled together and went to them. She instructed Achino'am to check on Amnon and see how he was faring.

"Do you know where Tamar is?" She asked Abigail who did not. She then found Ma'acah and inquired if she knew where her daughter Tamar was. She did not, but joined her in the search, reading the concern in Bathsheba's voice. They found her in a small room of Ma'acah's chamber, wailing and shaking like a leaf in the wind. Ma'acah ran to her.

"My daughter! What troubles you?" Tamar turned to see the open arms of her mother and ran to them, collapsing in a heave of wailing. Ma'acah stroked her hair and waited patiently as Tamar tried to catch her breath. She saw Bathsheba standing behind her mother and tore herself from Ma'acah's embrace.

"He . . . he. . . ." She covered her mouth and shook her head violently.

"What did he do?" Bathsheba asked quietly and took a tentative step toward her.

Ma'acah looked from Tamar to Bathsheba. "Who? What are you talking about?"

"I saw her coming from Amnon's chamber." Bathsheba told her. Ma'acah nodded. "Achino'am said he had been ill, and her father David instructed her to go to and make some cakes to cheer him." Bathsheba looked to Tamar who was still sobbing loudly in a heap on the floor.

"Did you go see Amnon tonight?" Bathsheba asked. Tamar just nodded. Ma'acah asked Bathsheba to look after Tamar as she got word to the king. When her mother had left the room, Tamar went to Bathsheba and fell into her arms travailing loudly. She would not speak of what happened and would not be consoled. She pushed herself out of Bathsheba's arms and went over to one of the torch plates that caught the ashes from past fires. She began placing the ashes on her head, as a girl in great mourning. Bathsheba recognized the pattern, like a lamb to the slaughter. She had worn the same expression of a woman caught in the lust of a man. She could not imagine what her brother Amnon had done to her.

Her wails were loud and echoed down the palace walls.

"Child, be silent!" Bathsheba begged her but it was too late. The door to the chamber opened with a bang and David strode into the room, his cloak flapping wildly behind him. Ma'acah followed him into the room, worriedly wringing her hands nervously. She was trailed by Achino'am who looked frightened.

"Tamar. What has happened? Why are you in such distress?" he demanded, hands on hips. Bathsheba went into protection mode and rose to meet her husband. Tamar remained prone on the floor, her sobs causing her body to writhe on the floor. "She has been attacked by someone she should have trusted." David rudely pushed Bathsheba aside and focused his attention back to Tamar.

"Rise, daughter and speak. What is this about you being attacked?"

Tamar could only rise to her knees and grasped her father's garments as if to stabilize herself.

"Father, father, I beg for justice. I am soiled, unclean before my God and thrown aside as carelessly as if I were trash!" David's eyes grew wide at the word 'unclean.'

"What are you talking about? Who said you were unclean?"

"Amnon, sir. It was Amnon who caused me to . . . to feel so, so . . . *dirty!*"

David straightened in indignation. He exchanged looks with Bathsheba and they silently recalled the prophet Nathan's prophecy. It echoed in Bathsheba's head no matter how hard she tried to erase it from her mind. *"The sword will never depart from your house because you despised the Lord and took the wife of Uriah to be your own."* He strode out of the room with as much force as he entered and left the women alone. Achino'am looked back and forth from Bathsheba to Tamar to Ma'acah trying to meet someone's gaze. Abigail stood right behind her for moral support.

"Do something!" Achino'am cried to no one in particular. A frightened bleat escaped from her mouth as she fled from the room, followed by Abigail. Ma'acah's eyes followed her out. They grew dark with anger and her hands formed fists. She looked back at Tamar and held her in an stare that communicated more coldness than comfort. She leered at Bathsheba who had gathered Tamar back in her arms.

Ma'acah cleared her throat. "I must go investigate these accusations with my son, Absolom and with Achino'am. Please stay with Tamar and comfort her while I am gone."

Bathsheba nodded and tried to get the teenager in her arms to stop shaking like a leaf. The night seemed to never end.

"Shhhh, Tamar. Take a deep breath."

"He raped me, Bathsheba! He raped me."

"I know, child. I know." The tears began to flow down Bathsheba's cheeks. "I'm here. Shhhhhh. I'm here." She began to rock Tamar in her arms like she was a young girl. Bathsheba squeezed her eyes closed tight and tried to block out the pitiful wail that was escaping from Tamar. It sounded like a lamb let to the slaughter.

The next day, David instructed Amnon to see him in an official hearing. He instructed his scribes to be nearby to take down testimony. Bathsheba took her place in the royal court as she did on that day when the prophet Nathan had declared God's judgement. The other wives sat nearby. Bathsheba noticed Tamar on the side, eyes still puffy from a sleepless night of tears, but quiet. Amnon stood before his father, hands clasped behind his back.

"How are you feeling, Amnon?" David asked him with great self control. Bathsheba noticed the fire in his eyes and was surprised that arrogant Amnon could not read it.

"Better, father."

"You did not come to Solomon's celebration that your brother Absalom held in his honor last night."

"I was not feeling well, father." Amnon answered meekly.

"I understand Jonadab your cousin came to see you as well?"

"Yes sir."

"I do not recall seeing him at Solomon's party either."

"Jonadab was trying to cheer me up, sir."

"And when Achino'am asked me to send Tamar, did she cheer you as well?"

Amnon shot a look at Tamar. David slapped his hands angrily on the arm of his throne which caused Absalom who had been watching nearby to jump to his feet.

"Son, tell me what happened last night when Tamar brought you cakes."

"I loved Tamar, Absalom's sister. I was sick in my love for her."

"What happened!?"

"I was intoxicated by her beauty . . . and . . ."

"Tamar is also *your* half-sister!" David boomed. "I instructed her to cheer you with her food, do you dare incriminate me, your father and your king in your lust? I take no responsibility in this shameful act! Tamar!"

Bathsheba looked at Tamar who shook more violently at the sound of her father calling her name. She went to the girl and helped her rise. She continued to hold Tamar, giving her courage to speak.

"What happened in Amnon's quarters?" David asked her. Bathsheba gave her a squeeze.

"He needs to hear it again for the official record." She whispered in the girl's ear. "Answer child."

Tamar looked up meekly and caught Amnon's hateful gaze. "I made him cakes as you requested last night but he refused to eat them. He instead asked me to accompany him to the bedroom so that he may eat the cake from my hand."

David's angry stare shot from Tamar back to Amnon who still stood before him.

"Go on."

Tamar licked her lips and looked to Bathsheba who nodded and continued. "He took hold of me and wanted to lie with me. I begged him not to force me to do so. Where could I take my shame? Although I am his half sister, I asked him to seek my hand in marriage from you, father so that I may be taken with dignity."

"I will *kill* you!" Absalom screamed as he jumped in place. His mother Ma'acah rose in concern, and Achino'am also stood to her feet, terrified of what she just heard. Bathsheba looked around the room at the scene. What a den of wickedness this was! Certainly this is the sword that Nathan had prophesied to David that would never leave his house those years ago when he judged David's actions toward her. Dear God, what would you have us do now?

She looked to David, horrified, expecting him to pronounce a judgement. He instead ordered Absalom and his other wives to be removed from the proceedings. Amnon looked down at his feet. Tamar was shedding fresh tears as Bathsheba continued to have her arm around her for maternal support.

"Amnon," David began with great self control in his voice. "Do you still love Tamar and seek her to be your wife?" Amnon looked at Tamar again and the disgust in his gaze would not be hidden. Not waiting for a response, David asked Tamar. "Would you still have him as a husband? The law of Moses prohibits siblings from marriage."

"Yes father, what you speak of is true. I just wanted to get away from him. For as much desire as he had for me last night, after the act, he simply put me out, commanding his servant who attended him to bolt the door behind me as I left. I begged to be his bride only to redeem such a repulsive situation. I am no longer a maid! A payment — a *mohar* — a price for a bride must be paid to compensate for this! I am no longer able to marry another!!"

Bathsheba felt the bile rise in her throat as she heard Tamar tell her story. She could remember all too well how soiled she felt when lust had overtaken her as well. But to have been a virgin on top of that shame? Bathsheba felt for her so and wondered how David would react.

"I *hate* you, you whore!" Amnon screamed at her. "I will have you killed for your sin!" Achino'am put her arm out to try and reason with her son who had forgotten where he was. Ma'acah cried out for justice for her daughter and made a move toward Achino'am who met her aggressiveness with a hearty shove that sent Ma'acah sprawling on the ground. The fire that was in David's eyes rose from within his throat in a guttural shout that quieted the room.

"AHHHHH!"

Wearily, King David sank back into his throne. He ordered Amnon to be taken to his quarters with guards by the door as he sought the Lord's counsel in this matter. He asked Bathsheba to take Tamar back to her quarters. Ma'acah tried to protest but David insisted he wanted to speak with her. As they left the room, Bathsheba noticed David call Nathan over to him for counsel. When she brought a tearful Tamar home, Absalom was there, pacing in front of the door.

"What did Amnon do to you, sister? Has he been with you?" Absalom rushed her before Tamar could go inside. Bathsheba quietly intervened. "Perhaps this isn't the time, Absalom."

"Come to my quarters, sister." Absalom coaxed. "Our mother Ma'acah is there and we can take care of you until we hear from father." Bathsheba looked at Tamar who nodded timidly. She allowed to be taken by her brother and remained desolate. Quietly, Bathsheba returned to her own home and sank to her knees. She cried out to God, wondering why Solomon's birthday celebration had to be clouded by such family turmoil. She prayed for justice. For God to grant David wisdom. She began to sob for Tamar and wondered where God had been when Amnon took her.

CHAPTER TWELVE

The days seemed to pass slowly. Although David was clearly angry at Amnon and was rethinking the order of succession on who would inherit his throne, he did nothing to correct Amnon or to further protect Tamar. He was not seen in court for many days. None of the wives had audience with him and the whole palace seemed to be in a worthless holding pattern. For his part, Absalom was playing it cool. When Bathsheba asked how Tamar was doing, his comfort for his sister continued for her mourning was great. He did not speak good or bad of his brother, Amnon, but had his heart set on revenge since his father was doing nothing.

Achino'am knew better than to defend her son against such a heinous act and settled into a meek cooperation among David's wives. Even Abigail who had been so stalwart in her defense for Achino'am did not argue that a great sin has been committed within the household of King David. Without a formal pronouncement from him, the women were unsure how to treat Achino'am and Bathsheba felt a little sorry for her to be treated like such an outsider. She noticed that David did not request audience with Achino'am and the two of them hadn't taken one of their evening walks in weeks. The months turned into years and the palace hoped time would put the sordid past behind them.

Solomon had learned to walk and was a happy toddler. He was a delight to Bathsheba's days. He would coo and gurgle at the birds that flew past his window, or bang on his plate with the little spoon of his. With Achino'am and Abigail distancing themselves from Bathsheba, another one of David's wives, Abatal, was Bathsheba's companion in recent days. Her son Chilean would play with Solomon and the four of them would pass the hours together. They would often go to the river's edge and let the children splash in the water much to the annoyance of the maidens that would accompany them on such outings. Bathsheba would use this time to do some laundry, continuing to keep Tamar in prayer and wondering when the situation would have any sense of closure. She missed seeing her young friend who had lived in virtual seclusion since the attack.

One day, she was sitting in the hall mending one of Solomon's tunics. He had tripped and tore a hole at the knee. Her servant Rachel had offered to do the work for her, but Bathsheba liked doing these small household chores. It reminded her of simpler times before she was a queen. She felt a presence near her and looked up. Tamar was hiding behind a fern, watching her. Bathsheba smiled at her and put the mending to the side. Resting her hands in her lap, she waited patiently for Tamar to draw closer.

The teenager sat quietly beside Bathsheba and she put a maternal arm on her shoulders.

"I have missed seeing you, Tamar. How have you been."

"The days pass."

Bathsheba shook her head and recognized the danger of Tamar falling into a deep depression. She knew what it was like for a man to take advantage her. Bathsheba whispered. "But our God is bigger and calls us to forgive."

Tamar recoiled from her as if she had just produced a hissing cobra. "I could *never* forgive Amnon!"

"Yes, I have felt that way too. I used to think if I allowed forgiveness to soften my heart, it would be like I was condoning the wrong that was done to me."

"Yes!" Tamar cried. "I must remember so perhaps someday he will pay for what he did to me."

"I have learned that forgiveness is not the same thing as approval. Staying angry at someone and refusing to forgive is like drinking a goblet of poison and waiting for the other person to die." Bathsheba pointed out gently. "Forgiveness is not easy. It is not a quick fix or cheap grace, especially after how you have been violated, Tamar. That will *never* be okay. Forgiveness comes from Jehovah and it says that God is bigger than the person who offended us."

Bathsheba waited as her words sunk in. She didn't want to hurt Tamar, but her isolation was like a cancer eating her up from the inside. Tearfully, Tamar looked at her.

"How do you do that?"

Bathsheba smiled encouragingly. "One day at a time. You have had your season of grieving. Don't give Amnon any more power over you." Bathsheba gently lifted Tamar's chin with her hand and lifted her own head as well.

"Remember, you are royalty. You are the daughter of King David and one of God's chosen people. Hold your head high. God will restore your dignity." Tamar's brow furrowed like she didn't believe it.

"The choice is yours. What will you do, Tamar?"

"I don't want to feel like a victim anymore." she whimpered.

"Then don't act like one anymore. God has seen your pain and it not finished with your story yet. Your father, my husband,

King David wrote a Psalm about this and I memorized the words and they have encouraged me. Would you like to hear it?"

Tamar wiped her face and nodded.

Bathsheba nodded and looked off into the distance.

"I will lift up mine eyes unto the hills, from where does my help come? My help comes from the Lord which made heaven and earth. He will not let you foot slip."

Bathsheba looked back at Tamar and held her gaze as she recited the next part of David's psalm.

"He who watches over you and all of Israel will never sleep. He is the shade at your right hand so the sun will not harm you by day nor the moon by night. The Lord will keep you from all harm and He will watch over you your entire life. He will notice your coming and going both now and forevermore."

"That is beautiful." Tamar murmured.

"I believe it to be true. We serve a just God. Don't worry about the consequences coming to Amnon. Vengeance belongs to God. You need to get back to believing that you are a worthy maiden."

Tamar grasped her hands. "Thank you, Bathsheba. I can't talk to anyone else like I do with you. You have encouraged my heart. It will take some time, but if you continue to remind me, I think I can learn to forgive."

"That's our girl." Bathsheba smiled. "Now go. I am sure you have something more interesting to do than mending a tunic." She picked up her sewing again and watched the girl leave.

"Watch over her, Adonai. She will need your strength in the coming days." Bathsheba whispered to the empty hall. Her eyes fell back on the project in her lap and began pulling the needle and thread, lost in thought and prayer.

CHAPTER THIRTEEN

A full two years later, Absalom announced he was hosting another feast. It was during the sheep harvest festival, when the shearers were in town and the wool was being harvested and dyed. Bathsheba was with Ma'acah separating the fluffy wool into bags when Absalom walked past.

"My son, what is this I hear of a celebration?" Ma'acah asked him.

"It has been a long time since merriment filled the halls. I asked my father if I could host a celebration feast for all the king's sons. Bathsheba, you may bring Solomon if you'd like. You too, Abatal. Bring Chileab. All of the king's children are welcome." Bathsheba nodded her consent as her hands continued to work. She exchanged a look with Abatal who shrugged slightly.

"It makes my heart happy son, that you have found reason to make merry again."

"How is Tamar?" Bathsheba asked him.

Absalom looked at her and for a split second, she thought a glint of anger flashed from his eyes. He smiled and said "She will be at the banquet as well." This didn't really answer Bathsheba's question and she had missed spending time with Tamar as they used to do but didn't press Absalom for she knew that his words were dismissing any further discussion on the matter. She spied Solomon playing nearby and smiled as she watched him follow a tuft of wool dance in the afternoon breeze. He tried to chase it on his wobbly toddler legs, but fell more times than he stepped. It would be good to attend a party. Solomon always liked the music. Bathsheba was hopeful once again.

Her servants helped brush her hair for the occasion a week later. Absalom in true form had assembled all the finest for the feast. The decorations hung festively from the eaves and the banquet table was full of the most delicious delicacies. Bathsheba had Solomon propped on her hip and was bouncing him with the rhythm of the harpist. He threw his head back a giggled. She smiled back at him and nuzzled her nose against his chubby skin. It was sticky from a cake he had firmly in his hand. She had been searching for Tamar but it took a great while for Bathsheba to finally spot her sitting quietly in a corner. She made a beeline for her across the room.

"Hello Bathsheba." The two women hugged in greeting.

"Oh, Tamar. How are you faring?"

"My brother Absalom has been very generous to me."

"This celebration is quite generous." Tamar merely nodded. Bathsheba wasn't sure it was in agreement.

"And Amnon? Has he bothered you any more?"

"No. With as much lust as he displayed for me, masquerading it as love, he now has such hatred as that of a righteous man toward a harlot, he despises me so."

"Tamar . . ."

"Please." She held up a hand to silence Bathsheba. "I have had my fill with all the kind words from others. They don't really understand. I am trusting that God will deliver my justice. One day at a time, right?"

Bathsheba smiled. "Right." She marveled at how she had matured in the past two years since the incident. Such a tragedy had thrust her from adolescence into the cold reality of adulthood in record time.

"As you wish. No more talk of your well being." Bathsheba smiled. Solomon began to clap his hands, his cake forgotten and in crumbles all over the floor. Tamar laughed. "Solomon has grown into such a handsome boy." He giggled as though he understood her words.

"Would you mind taking him for a moment? I'd like to get another glass of wine." Bathsheba passed Solomon to Tamar's arms where he began to play with the ringlets in her hair. She hoped her son would cheer Tamar. Turning, she went to the wine steward and waited as he poured her a glass. She overheard Absalom standing nearby with two of his servants.

"Continue to make Amnon's heart merry with wine. Then meet me outside like we planned."

Bathsheba shot a look to the head table where Amnon was slurping up another drink from his goblet. It spilled down his cheek a bit but he didn't bother wiping it off. He teetered a bit and continued with a conversation he was having. What was Absalom planning? Perhaps his heart wasn't as forgiving of his brother's grievance as he would like us all to believe. She took her own cup of wine from the steward, glancing back at Solomon and Tamar. The two of them were still playing together so she decided to follow Absalom instead.

The party crowd slowed her progress and she could not cross the room fast enough, but saw Absalom's servants lead a drunk Amnon out the back door. Absalom was nowhere to be found. Bathsheba knew that King David in his sadness, had declined to attend the banquet, obviously oblivious to the mayhem that was building between his sons. She wished he was here with her now for he would know what to do with the mounting tension. There was a commotion in the crowd as the king's sons,

Daniel, Adonijah, Sephatiah and Abital noticed the absence of Absalom and Amnon. They rushed outside, mounted their horses and rode off into the night. Bathsheba watched as the cloud of dust settled from the retreating hoofbeats. She turned back to the celebration and noticed it was decidedly over.

"Where have David's sons gone?" Abigail asked her. Bathsheba shook her off and boldly went off to speak with the king. It took awhile amid all the people to get permission from the royal guard, but was eventually led to a balcony where David was witnessing the departure of his sons on horseback.

"Did you find it wise allowing Amnon to attend Absalom's party? The trouble between them was severe. I wish you had come to the celebration tonight."

David looked to the horizon where he sons had ridden off. "I questioned Absalom but he insisted. I thought it for the best. Perhaps they had found an agreement."

"Absalom is not one to forget a grudge, especially one involving his sister, Tamar."

"I have not forgotten what happened, Bathsheba."

"But you also *did* nothing! It was as if you condoned the act. That is what a weak man does."

Angrily, David spun to face Bathsheba. "You are forgetting your place. Amnon is my *son!*" Courageously forging ahead, Bathsheba felt she could not stay silent now. "She is your *daughter!* A full two years have passed without any judgement from you, the king." He spun around and flew down the stairs and into the banquet hall with Bathsheba close on his heels.

With many of the hosts of the feast departed, the party crowd began to disperse, returning to their homes with such an anticlimactic ending to such a celebration. Somewhere from inside the hall, a table was upset. The crash of pottery and glass could be heard on the marble palace floor. Both Bathsheba and

David turned to go back inside when another horse and rider approached with such tenacity, it caused David to pause.

"Sire! I beg your audience." He dismounted from his horse with such haste the horse reared a bit on its hind legs. Jonadab, son of David's brother appeared out of the crowd to calm the beast.

"Whoa, girl." Jonadab patted the mare's nose and called for a steward to take her to the stables. He came up to David and Bathsheba at the same time as the messenger.

"Absalom has killed all the king's sons! Not a one of them is left!"

Bathsheba heard a scream and realized it came from her own mouth. David began tearing his clothes as a man in mourning. Bathsheba turned to him and ranted, "Why do you travail like a man who has lost everything? Will you not confirm this message? You are quick to accept it as truth!" Realizing she was still holding her cup of wine, she threw it on the ground just missing Jonadab's boot. Wine and pottery shards splattered on the ground. This caused people around them to stop and stare.

David took Bathsheba's arm at the elbow and turned to go back to the private quarters.

"We will *not* do this under the open air." He hissed. The messenger and Jonadab followed quickly behind them. He walked to a small annex room off of the celebration hall. Servants stood ready nearby. Bathsheba's mind was reeling. As a young man, David had committed adultery with her, tried to get her husband Uriah drunk and then had him murdered. Tonight, history repeated itself. David's son had raped his daughter, and now their brother had tried to get him drunk and now this; news of more murder!

"Sir, take heart. This report is not accurate. Not all of your sons are dead. Only Prince Amnon. Absalom slew him in vengeance for his sister Tamar's honor." A servant reported. Jonadab looked at him with distaste, and strode toward him menacingly, hands on hips. "You question the validity of my report?"

"Nephew, we both know it is over exaggerated, yes." David took a few paces toward Jonadab, asserting his authority. The servant meekly responded as he respectfully kept his head low before his king and backed up, giving himself space from Jonadab. Arrogantly, Jonadab stood his ground and looked David straight in the eyes.

David fiercely struck Jonadab. The force of the blow sent him rolling on the ground. Bathsheba jumped back and the messenger stood speechless. Holding his jaw, Jonadab looked up at the king with the same angry frown he had given the messenger. Hearing the commotion, other wives ran into the room. Breathless Abigail followed by Achino'am.

"Weren't you the one who initially went to cheer Amnon in his illness?" David roared at Jonadab. "And when you were not able to do so, you called for Tamar? Now do you seek my good graces for being the bearer of such news that you call good? You didn't even speak truthfully!" David turned to the other messenger. "Go speak with my first officer, Joab. I need to know how many of my sons are slain." The messenger nodded and hurried off as Jonadab staggered to his feet, rubbing his chin.

"As for you," David stood facing his nephew. "You have acted treacherously. You are not an ally to this kingdom nor a friend to my son. Guards!" Armed sentinels that were ever standing in the doorway immediately moved to his side. "Arrest this man!" Achino'am gasped as Abigail brought her hand to cover her mouth. Bathsheba stood frozen, watching the entire scene.

"Uncle!" Jonadab's anger morphed into incredulous fear as the guards each seized an arm and lifted Jonadab so that only his toes drug on the ground as they hauled him away to prison. "Uncle!" He cried out again. David raised his hand, instructing the guards to pause. Jonadab jumped on his chance. "You are correct. My first report was not accurate. It is only Amnon who was slain. Be of good cheer, for your other sons fare well." He tried to smile meekly. David went to him and went nose to nose.

"How dare thee tell me to be merry! This changes nothing! One son, all my sons, the detail matters not! The palace has suffered a death! Succession has been interrupted. How is it that *you* know this bit of information? I do not trust you, you snake! Take him away!" The guards disappeared with Jonadab, still pleading for mercy. Bathsheba stood motionless, trying to make sense of what just happened. With a defeated sigh, David looked to the ground.

"Are you happy wife? I *did* something about the situation." He walked to Achino'am. "You son has caused great strife in the household!" He spun and stomped out of the room. Achino'am crumpled into a sobbing ball on the floor, being supported only by Abigail who was whispering soothing words to her. Bathsheba slowly went out to the now deserted celebration hall. Distracted, she began to pick up items off the floor and put them on a nearby table. A bowl, a goblet, bits of meat. Wiping her hands on her tunic. She looked around the room and sighed. Adonai, what would you have us do now? Once again, she felt very alone.

CHAPTER FOURTEEN

B am, bam, bam! The knock on the door was insistent. Bathsheba rose from her bed and wiped sleep from her eyes. The visitor would not be ignored. Bathsheba was tying a tunic about her, shaking off her foggy head from sleep and walking to the front room as one of her maidservants opened the door to a very distraught Ma'acah. She looked past the servant and ran straight to Bathsheba.

"Have you heard from him?" she pleaded grabbing Bathsheba's elbows.

"Who?"

"My son, Absalom! He has not been home for three days now. Ever since the party last weekend. Word is he has fled from his father's wrath. Have you heard from him?"

"No, Ma'acah. I have not."

Ma'acah crumpled to the floor and began to wail. "First Tamar, now Absalom! Why does God hate my children so?" Bathsheba knelt beside her. "Shhhh, Ma'acah. I understand your grieving mother's heart. How I wish I could find words of comfort for you."

Ma'acah looked into Bathsheba's eyes with a tear stained face. "If Absalom never returns I shall not be able to bear it!"

Suddenly, a shout could be heard from outside the palace walls.

"They are coming!" They are coming!"

Bathsheba quickly threw a shawl on her shoulders and ran a comb through her hair. She was walking quickly down the palace halls and were soon joined by more of David's wives, Michal, Abatal, Abigail and Achino'am. Ma'acah was tearfully following as well. The women went together to a balcony and noticed riders coming toward the city gates in a cloud of dust. David was already outside to meet them, followed by his nephew, Jonadab who had spent a night in prison when Absalom first disappeared. As the riders approached, Bathsheba began to recognize some of David's sons. Adonijah, Haggish's son, reached his father first. He dismounted his horse and embraced David. Abigail's son, Shephatiah, and Ithream, Eglah's boy, joined them. The men were huddled and spoke in hushed tones.

David suddenly lifted his head toward the sky and let out a loud wail. He tore his cloak and wept. His sons grabbed his arms to support him and the men moved into the palace. Bathsheba quickly instructed one of her servants to go find out what the trouble was as she and the other wives waited anxiously. Soon, the servant returned and bowed reverently.

"Sir, word is that Absalom has fled to his mother's homeland of Geshur upon killing his brother Amnon for the rape of his half-sister, Tamar.. David is mourning Absalom's absence." Bathsheba nodded that she had heard and turned to Achino'am who had begun to wail for her son.

"Achino'am, be happy that he is safe and alive! Be happy in that for now." Bathsheba advised her.

As the days passed, much of the palace mourned for handsome Absalom. He was charismatic and well liked among many of the palace inhabitants and few could understand why he had fled so suddenly. Bathsheba made a point to go talk with Tamar one afternoon. She had been laying low during all the tension, so Bathsheba intersected her at the water well.

"How have you been, Tamar?"

Tamar's tough facade seemed to fade at the compassionate words of her friend. Her shoulder's sagged as her eyes grew wet.

"I didn't think I could possibly cry any more. It's been awful. I spend my days trying to keep busy and not run into Achino'am. She is so sad over the death of her son, but I cannot help but feel grateful to Absalom for defending my honor so." She wiped a tear that had begun to roll down her flushed cheek. Her finger left a dusty trail on her face. "Still, I cannot be happy for Absalom is not here with us. He fled out of fear of what father will do. Mother is beside herself and all the energy she put in my recovery is now spent in worry over Absalom's well-being."

Bathsheba had set her water jug down and was absent-mindedly tugging on the well's rope for water just to keep her hands busy as she listened.

"I fear Adonai shall never provide me with a husband! Who would have a soiled dove like me? I am unclean just as our ancestor Tamar whom I am named after. Judah had taken her, thinking she was a prostitute when he would not provide her a son to marry in her widowhood."

Bathsheba nodded, she had heard the oral story passed down of the twelve tribes as well. Judah had sinned with his daughter in law just as Amnon sinned with his sister. She couldn't help recalling the faint memory of David calling her to his quarters when she was newly married to Uriah. Do all men behave on the impulses of their flesh? Jehovah God, wilt you not be with your women who strive to serve you?

"I have no comforting words for you, Tamar except what I know in my heart to be true. God is a mighty God who sees all our tears and He is also just. In this unfortunate circumstance, we need to cling to His promises. It is all we have. Know that you are not alone. I too have fallen prey to the hands of a lustful man. Remember, I know how you feel."

Tamar's eyes flew open wide with question that Bathsheba silenced with her hand. "I will not speak of it anymore, just know that you are not a soiled dove. God will work it out." She lifted her now full water jug and instructed Tamar to do the same. "Wipe your tears and let's get home. Hold your head high and serve diligently as one who knows Jehovah God." The two women slowly retraced their steps from the well back to the security within the palace.

A few weeks later, David called for a day of remembrance for his sons. He was pained with the knowledge that Amnon was dead for his awful deed toward his sister Tamar, but knew that it was just. He was grieved for Absalom who had still not returned to the palace. David stood and faced the crowd. The wives were seated on either side of him, sons and other children also nearby.

"God had told me, some time ago through his prophet Nathan, that the sword would not depart from my house because of my transgressions. Our God is just but my distress is severe. Let us pray to our God for repentance and the safe return of Absalom.

"Turn Thou to me and be gracious to me, for I am lonely and afflicted, oh God. Relieve the troubles that overtake my heart and bring me out of this darkness. Consider my great affliction and troubles and please forgive me of my sin. Transgression speaks to the wicked deep in his heart. There is no fear of God before his eyes. Thy judgements are like the great deep, you saves man and beast, Oh God."

Later than night, David was in Bathsheba's chamber, anxiously pacing before the window.

"Husband, you must get some rest. Israel will not fare well with an exhausted ruler." Bathsheba's words sounded flat to her own ears but she felt compelled to fill the silence. David would not be consoled.

"David . . ." she said softly. At the sound of a more intimate tone, with formalities put aside, David turned toward Bathsheba.

"How can I have peace? Somewhere out there, Absalom roams. He has the very same defects of character which I myself had to master, but I fear that these detriments will run wild in my son and it will be the end of him. The gracious Lord has indeed granted me forgiveness for taking you from Uriah and blessed us with another son, Solomon. But the consequences of those choices all those years ago! They still reap a bitter harvest."

Bathsheba knew how a parent's heart grieved for a child. She remembered well the ache in her heart when her first child died so soon after birth. Like David, she was steadfast in her trust in Almighty God and knew in her heart of hearts that he had not forgotten them. How she wished she could say something to bring cheer to David. He had stopped pacing and came to sit next to her on the bed. He stroked the hair near her face.

"Out of all my wives, I knew you would understand my pain for Absalom. That is why I needed to be here with you tonight. Ma'acah is too caught up in grief. How I wish I knew what the Lord was going to do." He slumped off the bed onto his knees and fell face first on the ground. Bathsheba dared not move. Not many people were allowed to witness the king in such a vulnerable and weak state.

"My God, my God!" David wailed. Bathsheba drew her robe up about her and brought her clenched hands to her mouth to suppress a whimper. "How long wilt thou have your servant writhe under the force of thine judgement? *Rebuke me not in thy anger, nor chasten me in thy wrath! For thy arrows have sunk into me and thy hand has come down on me. There is no soundness in my flesh because of Thine indignation. There is no health in my bones because of my sin. For my iniquities have gone over my head, they weigh like a burden too heavy for me!* Oh my God, I am drowning!"

Bathsheba recognized one of the poems David penned, he had recited it to her before. But David did not stop there, he spoke on of his devotion and obedience even though the circumstances did not look good. "*I delight to do thy will, Oh my God.*" David whispered, drawing himself up to a sitting position on the floor. "*I have not concealed thy steadfast love and thy faithfulness from all my kingdom. You are my refuge and my strength. My very help in times of need.*"

Bathsheba's stance relaxed in the presence of her husband's resolve. David was a good man with a good heart. Yes, Jehovah. Bathsheba silently agreed with her husband. Please show us your will and we will walk in your way.

CHAPTER FIFTEEN

Three more long years passed without a word from Absalom. Solomon had begun school with the royal teachers with the rest of David's children. He was a quick learner and enjoyed engaging in the physical games they boys played after lessons.

Joab, one of David's most trusted commander's in his army, had sought audience with her one afternoon. She agreed to hear him out, in the presence of her handmaidens in the garden on one of the terraces that overlooked Jerusalem. As he entered, he paused a moment and bowed low.

"My Queen."

"Good tidings, Joab. You asked to see me?" Bathsheba asked, motioning for him to sit on a nearby bench. The jasmine was in bloom and Bathsheba watched the bees buzzing about the flowers as Joab obliged to sit beside her. He licked his lips before speaking.

"Yes, I have perceived that the king's heart is still grieving for Absalom. His absence has not been easy on the king."

"You are correct. He mourns day after day. The months have turned to years."

"I may know where Absalom is."

Bathsheba stood. "Do you? Why not call him home and ease his father's heart?"

Joab also stood and faced Bathsheba. Her handmaidens drew in a half circle behind her.

"You ask a political question. David's heart of a father would like nothing less than to call his son home with great jubilation. But, the fact of the matter is, Absalom is responsible for the death of his brother, Amnon and the law requires him to be severely punished by the king. David's position as ruler of the land prohibits him from acting upon his father's heart which longs for his son."

"What then shall be done?"

"I have an idea that came to me a week ago, and wondered if you could be of some assistance."

"Go on." Bathsheba said as she sat back down on the bench and absently began stroking a nearby fern with her palm.

Joab began to pace before her a bit as he explained his plan. "If we could have a spokesperson, someone who could get audience with the king and plead a case as a parent for a wayward child, perhaps David would see fit to call him home."

"But as you have said, Absolom did seek vengeance himself which the Lord God has instructed is to be for He and He alone."

"Yes, my Queen. You speak the truth. But this stalemate we have in the kingdom is to no advantage. The king in his misery has grown dull in his political duties and I fear could become vulnerable to our enemies. It must not be easy for Absolom to be out there living each day as a fugitive, wondering if your father will ever forgive you."

Bathsheba looked at Joab as he paused and returned her gaze. "Surely, King David knows how welcome forgiveness is."

"You are bold." Bathsheba replied softly.

"Yes, my queen. I do beg your pardon."

Bathsheba stood and walked a few paces herself, pondering what Joab had said. "You wanted my assistance?"

"Yes, I remember that you had lived in a small principality north of here before moving to the palace here in Jerusalem. I was wondering if you knew of anyone who could speak to this type of situation. To try to persuade the king into doing something to bring Absalom home for the healing of them both."

"What kind of person are you looking for?"

"One who would entice the most compassion. A beggar or widow, perhaps. Older in years and therefore dependent on the goodness of others."

"Why do you seek to find a person outside Jerusalem?"

"Perhaps it would be easier to keep the king's honor intact and the distance would make verification of her story less readily available."

"I see. Let me think on it tonight and I will send word of you tomorrow." Joab bowed again as he left and Bathsheba retreated to her chambers. It had been a long time since she remembered her hometown. She had remembered her parent's home and her friendship with Anna. *Anna!* The name rang anew in Bathsheba's mind. Would she be willing to assist her after all these years? She hastily sent a message with one of the merchants who were heading south the next morning asking Anna to come. She then sent word to Joab that she was willing to help him for the sake of her husband, King David. Reconciling with his son Absalom surely was part of God's plan. Had Adonai not forgiven them?

The weeks passed swiftly as Bathsheba anticipated seeing her old friend again. When she finally got word that travelers had entered the city gates from Tekoa, in the region of the tribe of Simeon in southern Israel, she ran out to the palace gate and searched the crowd for a familiar face. She saw a woman shuffling slowly with a head of grey hair. Her frail hands were clutching a small bag and her face was leathered by years in the sun. She raised her eyes and met the gaze of Bathsheba and a smile immediately spread across her face.

The women embraced. "Anna! How I have missed you!"

"Bathsheba, queen of Jerusalem!" Anna held her face in her hands.

Bathsheba shrugged. "One of them."

"God has blessed you. I am so thankful to travel to His Holy City to see you." She looked up at the palace. "It is so stunning, this home of yours!"

"Come." Bathsheba kept a protective arm around her as she walked Anna to the guest quarters. She had instructed her maids to have fruit and cakes ready as well as a jar of fresh water. Anna was thankful to get out of the sun and sat on a chair, trying to catch her breath. Bathsheba put a small plate together of figs and dates and placed it next to Anna. She wiped her hands on her tunic and sat down. The women enjoyed a moment of silence.

"I was sorry to hear of Benaiah's passing." Bathsheba started. Anna shrugged.

"Adonai blessed him with a long life. Our sons are grown and I have thirteen grandchildren!"

"Thirteen!"

"Yes. But the baby girl, the youngest is my favorite." Anna leaned in conspiringly. "I know you shouldn't have favorites, but Naomi is my little shadow. She is so quick at learning that she can make Sabbath cakes all by herself and she is only nine years old." Anna took Bathsheba's hands in hers. "How have you been? Do you like it here?"

Bathsheba smiled. "There was a time I thought I would never heal from my loss of Uriah, and then a child not long after that." Anna's face contorted with a frown at the news as she listened.

"I did not understand why you disappeared so suddenly after Uriah's death. Something didn't feel right."

Bathsheba shrugged and had to agree. "It wasn't good. But God is good, His grace and forgiveness exceeds all my expectations. David is a good man. He has repented to me and Adonai for his sin and we have a son named Solomon. Oh, Anna, I can't wait for you to see him! He is so handsome and carries this little drum with him everywhere he goes. He is a little younger than your granddaughter Naomi, but is already quick with lessons as well. He has many royal half siblings here."

"David has many children?"

"Yes, it is one of his eldest sons, Absolom, which you are here to help. He did a wicked thing in response to another wicked thing . . ." Bathsheba went on to fill her old friend in with the sad details of the Lord's discipline within the house of David as the prophet Nathan had foretold when he confessed of his sin. How God's forgiveness is real, but sometimes hard to taste amid the consequences of sin. Like Jacob in stories from the Torah, his deceit with his father to steal the birthright from his twin brother Esau came back to haunt him when his uncle Laban deceived him into marrying his daughter Leah when he really loved Rachel.

Anna rocked back and forth, listening with the ear of a wise woman who had seen much life. "After I got your message to come, I have thought and prayed over it my entire journey here to Jerusalem. I brought my mourning garment from when I lost Benaiah. When shall I meet with the king?"

Bathsheba smiled at the spunk of her old friend. "I have requested that you spend time with Joab. He is a commander in David's army and came up with this plan to cheer my husband's heart. He will help you decide what to say and will set up the appointment to have audience with the king."

The women embraced again. "It is so good to see you again. I will let you rest from your long journey for now and make sure that my servants bring you evening meal. Please let me know if there is anything you need."

Anna smiled and nodded as Bathsheba softly closed the door behind her. Seeing Anna gave Bathsheba a twinge of homesickness, for the life she had before Jerusalem's palace. For Uriah and dreams of the past. It was quickly replaced when she heard her son, Solomon calling her.

"Mama, Mama!" Smiling, she followed the sound.

CHAPTER SIXTEEN

Days later, Bathsheba was seated in her spot to David's left at court during proceedings. King David had summoned Joab who had a visitor for him to see. Bathsheba was glad David could not see her face as her eyes took in Anna in her mourning robe. She bowed respectfully and thanked David for his ear. He nodded and she fell to the ground.

"Oh, king. I beg your help."

"What is it?" David compassionately asked.

"My husband is dead. I have two sons who quarrel. How they carried on for years, it broke a mother's heart!" David was nodding in acknowledgement as Anna continued to lament for her fictitious feuding sons. "One day," she dramatically continued, "they were fighting in a field and one son struck the other in his anger! Now my entire family wants to disown me because I am assisting my son who killed his brother. How can I turn my back on him? How can I let him face his trial, knowing that the law demands that he be killed as well? This would surely be the end of me, with no husband, no sons to care for me. What shall I do?"

Bathsheba was touched by her tears and couldn't believe what a good actress Anna was. She felt a twinge of guilt but prayed that the means justified the end. Her goal was for reconciliation in David's home.

"Go back to your house and I will give an order concerning you." David instructed but Anna continued to plead her case.

"Oh, king, I cannot bring conclusion to this situation which has befallen on my family, which is why I traveled so far to seek your counsel. I will willingly take the guilt if you could graciously excuse the sentence on my offending son. My father's house will shoulder the shame and leave the king blameless in bestowing mercy in this matter. If the king does not act swiftly, I fear that it will be too late and that my entire family will implode from such animosity. I cannot lose the last son I have! Surely this is not the Lord's will, to destroy a home!"

David held up a hand and silenced her. "As the Lord lives, not one hair of your son shall fall to the ground. If anyone says anything to you, bring them to me. I give you my vow." David nodded, assuming this was the end of the matter and waited for the next person to come. Instead, Anna stood and silently gathered her mourning robe about her. Bathsheba was awed at her friend's courage.

"Pray, may your servant say one more thing, dear king?" Bathsheba shot a look to David who allowed a small look of confusion pass over his eyes.

He nodded and waved his hand before her graciously. "Speak."

"Why have you then done such a thing? For in giving me such a gracious decree for my son, you *do* blame yourself, for I understand that you have a banished son abroad who should be called home again, do you not?" There was a quiet collective gasp from those listening. Bathsheba looked over at Joab who wore a smug look of satisfaction.

"Now I have boldly come to speak for there are many people who care for you." Anna continued boldly. "They are afraid of a kingdom that cannot stand with such animosity and sadness hanging over it. It is time to put the past in the past. Inasmuch as you have pardoned my son, a murderer whom you do not know, it is so much better for this nation that your heir, Sire, be returned to his home with such clemency that will begin the healing process of all your people. Your people have told me that you are able to discern good from evil and the Lord is your God. May He be with you." Anna bowed respectfully and waited for David's response.

David glanced at Bathsheba and then looked to the ground as he thought. Bathsheba wrung her hands in her lap as a silent prayer was lifted from her quivering lips. The silence although brief seemed so deafening.

"You have spoken truth, Almighty God Himself must have revealed this to you so that you may boldly bring me a message that Adonai's servant needed to hear. Who informed you of these things?"

"Your commander, Joab, sir." David looked to Joab who had wisely changed his countenance to more of a humble servant.

David nodded in acknowledgement. "Yes, Absolom murdered his brother Amnon, but his banishment will never bring Amnon back. Absolom justly deserves to die for his crime, but I have hesitated from seeking him and carrying out justice, for he too is my son. For the ruin of his sister, which lay upon Amnon's head, Absolom's act of vengeance is a pardonable case. God's example of clemency to me, his servant and king of this nation causes me to give and restore favor on the son that I still have in Absolom."

David had Joab come stand beside Anna. He bowed respectfully before the king.

"I grant this. Joab, go and bring back my son, Absolom from where he is presently hiding. Tell him that his father, the king, forgives him and wishes to restore a relationship with him."

Joab fell to his knees and kissed the floor. "Thank you, my king. Today, I know that you have found favor in me, your servant and commander for you have granted our request."

David nodded and Joab led Anna from the room.

"Joab." David called after him. Joab turned. "Thank you. Leave for Geshur tonight and retrieve Absolom, but he is to come back to his own house and *not* come into my presence."

Joab nodded. "Understood, sir."

Bathsheba's eyes met Anna's just before she disappeared outside the court door. Bathsheba looked back at David who's confusion was replaced with a twisted countenance Bathsheba couldn't decipher. Perhaps he was relieved that Absolom was returning home and his grieving would cease. But in having his son back, he would have to confront the murderous deed that caused the death of his other son, Amnon. Once again, David was called out publicly as he was when Nathan pointed out his adultery with her, but to David's credit, he was humble enough to learn from God's direction and followed obediently while keeping his kingly dignity. Bathsheba knew that this in part what made his subjects so loyal to him. He truly did have a discernment of good and evil and God blessed him. This quality caused him to be a benevolent and mighty king that prospered in the sight of all his enemies.

Bathsheba glanced over at Tamar sitting nearby. Her mouth was open in surprise. Bathsheba went to her.

"Amnon is dead!" Tamar said as if Bathsheba hadn't heard.

"Absolom is coming home, this is good news, right?"

Tamar nodded. "I have missed my brother as my mother, Ma'acah has. I wonder how Achino'am will feel?"

"David said so himself. Bringing Absolom home won't bring Amnon back, but the healing process must begin." Bathsheba shuddered however when she recalled David's words, '*but he is not to come into my presence.*' Absolom would be back, but the healing process between father and son was still severely fractured. True healing would take more time.

CHAPTER SEVENTEEN

Another two full years passed. Solomon was now a boy of seven, continuing his lessons with Chileab and a private rabbi at the palace. He learned to read swiftly, and Bathsheba was so proud when he would read from the Torah. He was chosen one Sabbath to read a passage and Bathsheba watched from the women's court as he went to the platform, dwarfed by the priests and David surrounding him. He read from Moses' account with quiet dignity and it swelled Bathsheba's heart. Perhaps her son would succeed his father on the throne. David had started talking about wanting to rebuild God's temple and can called the people to begin bringing in gifts of gold that he stored for that future dream. Bathsheba remembered all the the prophet Nathan had told her. David was a man of war and the honor of building a temple for God would go to his offspring. But as a 'man after God's own heart,' David did not waste any time but did what he could by beginning to gather the items for the construction.

Bathsheba hadn't seen much of Absalom in those twenty-four months. He was not invited into the palace or audience with King David the entire time since he had returned. He was the talk of the town, however. Extremely handsome, with a full head of thick, wavy, black hair that he would vainly brush and cut regularly when the hair became too heavy to carry. The warm sun would cause him to sweat, and many would purchase a lock of his hair at a price. Soon many people had this talisman from Absalom and relished in the notion that they had a piece of the handsome prince who may one day be king. Absalom had a family of his own, three sons and a daughter, he had named Tamar, after his sister who had been raped by Amnon. She took after her father and was a stunning beauty to behold. Bathsheba watched in disgust as many a man looked upon her with lust in their eyes.

She had spoke with Ma'acah about it one day as the women were weaving.

"Are you happy to have Absalom home?" Bathsheba had asked her.

Ma'acah smiled and nodded. "The people seem to really love my son. They buy locks of his hair, they celebrate his return . . ." she paused and her brow furrowed. Bathsheba gently touched her friend's arm.

"What is it?"

"Absalom took his cues from the people. There is talk of his succession to the throne. Although grateful for sidestepping any judgement for the murder of his half brother, Amnon, Absalom has decided that his father, King David, is weak in matters that are too close to home. he sees David's silence as a sort of absolution, but I know that David has not forgotten."

Ma'acah's heart was torn between having her son home and knowing that the animosity between father and son was still brewing to a boiling point, and it frightened her. "Absalom resolved that when *he* took the throne, he would *never* display such vulnerability and indecisiveness. The years have strengthened this resolve and Absalom has decided that he has waited long enough."

"Long enough?" Bathsheba asked, her own heart now picking up on Ma'acah's apprehension.

"His mannerisms in the marketplace and places of worship since he had been home had given the impression that he had not been humbled with sorrow, but flagrantly talked of when he spoke to his father and when he would be welcomed back into the palace with full pardon." Ma'acah explained. Bathsheba shuddered at such arrogance for she knew firsthand the Lord would not abide with the haughty.

"And how is your relationship with Achino'am?"

Ma'acah shook her head. "She still does not speak to me. I think she finds it unfair that her son was murdered while mine still lives and yet, she forgets about the pain I bear for the injustice that her son Amnon did to my daughter, Tamar!"

Bathsheba shook her head. Sin brings such a darkness over men's hearts and the affects of it are long reaching.

"I fear he's going to do something dreadful." Ma'acah whispered.

"What do you mean?" Bathsheba asked. Ma'acah met her gaze.

"Absalom will not go on being loved by the people and ignored by his father much longer. He will do something that will draw much attention, but I don't know what."

The next day, Bathsheba took Solomon into the marketplace. She was so proud when he would meet the merchants and greet them with such a manner that seemed older than his years. She was bargaining with a man over a bushel of wheat for bread when a scream erupted.

"Help! Help!"

Bathsheba looked up and there was smoke on the horizon. Suddenly, people seemed to be swarming in the marketplace and many were running toward the smoke.

"Get water!"

"Looks like Joab's field!"

"We need more jugs! Quick, let's go to the well!"

Pandemonium seemed to erupt. Bathsheba stopped one man as he was running past. "What is the trouble?"

"Commander Joab's field is on fire. Word is the men of proud, lawless Absolom started the fire!"

"Absolom!" Bathsheba cried. She gathered up her purchases and hurried Solomon back to the safety of the palace. There was confusion there too. Ma'acah was running around trying to salvage her son's reputation.

"If only Joab had agreed to see Absolom when he requested audience!" She cried to anyone who would listen. Bathsheba asked where David was and found him on the roof, watching the fire.

Bathsheba met the sentinels at the door to the roof and asked if she could have audience with her husband. One left to announce her and she was soon escorted up the stairs.

"Husband?" Bathsheba quietly entered his presence. He turned and waved her in, giving permission to her to speak. She joined him at the railing, watching the people frantically trying to put out the fire.

"Was it Joab's field?"

David nodded. "I got word that it was indeed Absolom. What was he *thinking*?" He began to pace and filled Bathsheba in. "Joab came to me and told me that Absolom has wanted to speak with me, but Joab has ignored him several times, then he goes and burns a field!"

"Why do you suppose he wants audience with you so badly?"

"He wishes to be restored to the kingdom, I presume."

"That is Ma'acah thinks."

"What did she say?" David turned to look at Bathsheba and she was sorry she had said that outloud.

"Ma'acah noticed that Absolom thinks your silence exonerates him from any wrongdoing in Amnon's death, but your lack of lauding him upon his return has him seeking his place on the throne prematurely."

David growled. "And Joab ignored Absolom's requests to see me?"

Bathsheba nodded meekly. "Apparently."

David rubbed his forehead and sighed. "Joab has been with me many, many years. I have trusted him and he knows me and my intentions well. He knows I am still very cross with Absolom and requesting to see him would be a waste of time. But to burn a field? It doesn't help his cause any."

"What are you going to do?"

"I have agreed to speak with Absolom in the morning. I do not believe that he is repentant or sorry for anything at all. He wishes to be restored to the kingdom, yes. But my son is proud. I fear he harbors some ulterior motive." David looked towards the door and waved his hand. "The way that Ma'acah is carrying on, I feel she also knows that Absolom's heart is unclean. But if what you tell me is accurate, it is not wise for Absolom to try and succeed me!"

"I will pray Adonai grants you wisdom. How is Joab?"

David sighed. "Saddened at the loss of his field. Angry, the Absolom has the audacity to force his hand. Probably upset with me that I have not acted on this matter sooner but I will deal with him after I deal with my son."

David crumpled into a nearby chair and put his face in his hands. "Will this tension in my family ever end? God has been so gracious, but sometimes the weight of what I have done, in spite of the mercy I have received, seems like more than I can bear."

"God will give you the strength." Bathsheba offered. David smiled at her.

"I am thankful for you, wife. You are a woman of noble character." David sighed and rose to look out the window. "Oh, Absolom. Your pride shall be your downfall."

CHAPTER EIGHTEEN

The next day, Bathsheba took Solomon to go see the goat herders as they passed the city changing pastures. She needed respite from the tension within the palace walls. Solomon would giggle at all the goat bleats and liked when they stumbled over each other. Bathsheba was amazed how the shepherds could control such a flock with just a staff. What was it David had taught her? That the staff was both a tool of discipline and of protection depending on how the shepherd dealt with the sheep. She tried to imagine David as a young boy. He had told her of his boyhood profession in the fields while his older brothers had more prestigious jobs like a place in the army and serving in war. He had written one of his songs about his experience with the sheep and it was so lyrical, Bathsheba knew it by heart. It was a beautiful picture of her husband's heart for his God and he likened it to a shepherd.

"*The Lord is my shepherd, I shall not want or worry. He makes me lie down in the green pastures and leads me beside still waters. . . .*"

Bathsheba also knew that shepherds were not looked upon as men of stature. They were securely in at the bottom rung on the social status ladder, which always struck her as a bit odd. Without shepherds, how would people be able to purchase lambs for offerings in the Holy Temple? An offering to Jehovah for the forgiveness of sins is one of the most sacred, necessary acts a man could make. Why then should the supplier of such goods be thought of so lightly?

Stranger still were the ways of God. Her husband had spent a good portion of his adolescence as a shepherd, and yet God had elevated him to King. God does not see as a man sees, but past the outer appearance into the heart. She had heard these stories as well. The prophet Samuel was sent to David's father, Jesse to anoint a future king that God would reveal. Everyone thought it would be one of David's older brothers, so much that no one even bothered to call David home from the pastures until Samuel asked if there was another brother. Then there was that amazing tale of David killing a Philistine named Goliath! He had gone to the battle where his brothers were serving to bring them food and he heard the giant taunting Israel. David had recounted how he had successfully killed bears and lions when they had come to attack the flocks and he knew that God would be with him in slaying Goliath too.

Bathsheba shielded her eyes from the sun with her hand as Solomon clapped and laughed as the parade of bleating goats continued by below. She continued with her reverie. David had told her that although the army was afraid of Goliath, even King Saul was cowering and not knowing what to do, the Lord told David to take his shepherd's sling. His faith in God rallied him even when his brothers and the other soldiers mocked him. They didn't believe for a minute that David would be successful. Bathsheba shuddered. Why then did his brothers allow him to go out and meet Goliath if they were certain of his impending death? Bathsheba remembered how David had chuckled at the fact that he took five stones, ready and willing to use them all to fall Goliath. But God is his might, had Goliath fall at the first stone. Will you not then help your servant David again, Adonai? Bathsheba silently prayed for her husband's peace.

"Mama, mama!" Solomon was tugging at the seam of her tunic. Bathsheba's daydreams faded and she knelt down to face her son.

"Yes, Solomon, what is it?"

He pointed with a chubby finger. "Is that brother Absolom?" Bathsheba stood and looked in the direction he was pointing. She could hear his words to those who were passing through the city gate.

"Good man, what city are you traveling from?" Absolom was in fine form. He was clean and handsome as ever. Seemingly important, he was gleaning attention from all sides. The women were unabashedly swooning and the men seemed to shuffle for the chance to shake his hand.

"See that your claims for the king are well thought out, although he is a very busy man. I hope you have good accommodations here in Jerusalem. It may take you awhile to get an answer. There is no one who will have time for you. Oh, but if *I* were reigning over the land, I would make sure that you would get justice and would make time to hear you all."

What is he up to? Bathsheba wondered as she walked with Solomon by the hand through the gates. She heard a little applause to Absolom's political campaign but was greatly concerned that he was arrogantly getting the people to question David's rule and was swaying the people's loyalties to himself. Still, when she returned to the palace grounds she said nothing to David, it was not her place. She watched as Ma'acah relaxed with news that her son Absolom was growing in popularity when he had fled with such a cloud of suspicion so many years earlier. Achino'am seemed to sulk in the shadow of Absolom's political campaign. Bathsheba wondered when

David would act, but he continued to be frustratingly aloof as if ignoring it would make it all go away. David's failure to act actually worked in favor for Absolom. Without rebuttal, the people believed every word that dripped from the charismatic diplomat. His handsome features helped put Israel even more at ease in seeing Absolom as a true successor to the throne and there was talk of an upcoming revolt.

One night, as soon as she had fallen asleep, David stormed into her chambers.

"Bathsheba, get up. Wake Solomon and pack a few items. We must flee!"

Bathsheba sat up and wiped her eye. "What? Where are we going?"

"Absolom has turned the people against me. Joab and some of my other advisors have told me that he was gathered up men and chariots to take over the kingdom. He dispensed such swift and murderous justice on his own brother Amnon, I fear that he will have no problem doing harm to me, you or little Solomon."

"But you are the king! Certainly the people would not wish to see their king retreat in such fashion." Bathsheba countered.

"I fear it was a mistake to bring him home. I do not wish to have a showdown with Absolom and all his ranting as of late have turned many of my subjects against me. I leave to preserve the kingdom until reason returns to men's minds. We leave within the hour. See to it that you are ready." He left her chambers with a whoosh from his robe. Bathsheba stuck her head out the door and saw David's other wives shooing their children to flee.

"Abigail!" Bathsheba called. "Where are we going?"

"Our husband is trying to protect us from proud Absolom who wishes to be king. We must obey and flee if we are to live!"

"Is everyone going?"

Abigail shook her chestnut hair. "Ma'acah is staying in support of her son and David is leaving the concubines to keep the house in our absence. Achino'am is already packing. Hurry Bathsheba. We must go!"

Solomon had awoke with all the commotion and was seeking refuge behind his mother's legs. She flew back into her chambers and threw some personal items into a bag. Solomon watched somberly. Bathsheba paused a moment and took his boyhood face in her hands.

"It will be alright, my son. Adonai will lead us. Your father is a good man and listens to God's counsel. We are going on a little trip and will return home soon." She wasn't sure she believed what she was saying.

Solomon rubbed his eyes with his fists and nodded sleepily. Bathsheba stopped by Ma'acah's chamber.

"Won't you join us?"

"Why should I flee from my son? David has not yet pardoned him for restoring Tamar's dignity. Many feel he should be king." Ma'acah replied coldly. Bathsheba shifted Solomon in her arms as she saw Tamar appear from a shadow in the hallway.

"Mother, I would like to go." Tamar said timidly. Ma'acah turned incredulously. "You will not stay and support your brother?"

"It's not my fight, mother. I was victimized but would just as well like to move on with my life. I need a break from these walls; they feel like they will suffocate me if I stay any longer. Please give Absolom my love when you see him. I pray all can be worked out between him and father and we can return soon."

Ma'acah turned to Bathsheba with a pleading look. "Will no one stay in support for Absolom?"

"Ma'acah, you know that he speaks out of turn and does not honor his father the king." Bathsheba immediately handed Tamar her traveling bag. "I will take care of your daughter. She will bring me great comfort while we are away and help with the care of Solomon." Without waiting for official consent, Tamar followed Bathsheba out and joined the throng of David's household under the blanket of stars as they wordlessly left the safety of Jerusalem's gates. She gathered her tunic about her so her legs wouldn't get caught in it's folds as they climbed the hill toward the garden in the Mount of Olives. Bathsheba watched as one of David's mighty men came out from the crowd to greet her husband. He was one of thirty men who had fought before in King David's honor and was part of an honored guard.

"Sire. All your servants, wives save but Ma'acah and children have passed safely from the city walls. We also estimate six hundred Gittities who have served you loyally and still believe you to be God's anointed king for us." David embraced him mightily.

"Thank you, Ittai. Why do you also go with us? Like the crowd of Gittities, you are a foreigner and have no dog in this fight. Why not go home and be safe? Absolom has no qualm with you and here I flee, not yet knowing exactly where I am going to lay my head. May the Lord be faithful to you, for I know that your loyalties are with me."

Ittai shook his head and smiled. "Wherever you go, is where me and my family will call home. I have watched the Lord go with you and know that whatever happens, it is best to be with you." David smiled appreciatively and nodded in agreement. He wearily let Ittai pass and continued to walk away from his beloved Jerusalem. Bathsheba noticed the tears welling in his eyes that matched the lump in her throat. She paused and watched the throngs of people following them. This must have what it looked like when our ancestors fled Egypt for the wilderness. She noticed all the people began to weep and wail and she turned and continued her trek by her husband's side.

"After all this, I still love him." David said meekly. "How can I not love my son?" Bathsheba patted his arm, trying to encourage him.

"Your majesty!" They heard a call from behind them. David stopped and turned as a man Bathsheba knew as Zadok came running up.

"A few of us have taken the ark of the Lord with us as we flee. Shall we lead the procession?"

David shook his head. "Take the ark back to Jerusalem. If God is with us, and I still find favor in his eyes, we may return to Jerusalem and the ark. If however, I prove to be a coward and on a fool's errand with all my household, then let the Lord do with me what he will, here in the wilderness." Zadok's eyes searched David's for more explanation. He clearly did not understand what seemed to be defeat in the king's reasoning but obeyed. David watched him leave and sighed deeply. He raised his hands to cause the people to stop moving and listen.

"Before we travel any further, we need to pause and pray to God for direction. Join me, all those who trust in the Almighty. God of Abraham, Isaac and Jacob." David turned, and slipped out of his sandals. He covered his head and began to weep. Bathsheba held Solomon back who wanted to be held by his daddy.

"Fold your hands, Solomon. Daddy needs us to pray."

CHAPTER NINETEEN

The months passed slowly and Bathsheba couldn't remember being warm. She missed the palace and all its splendor, but also missed the sensation of security. She was not accustomed to living in tents out in the open. Just like a shepherd, she mused and remembered the day when she and Solomon had watched the goat herders.

She was sitting with David at breakfast one morning and he filled her in.

"A few weeks after we fled, I sent Hushai the Archite to return to Jerusalem under the guise of being loyal to Absolom. He is actually serving as my eyes and ears so that I may keep abreast of what is happening to my kingdom. Recently, one of his servants has returned to inform me that Absolom is playing right into our hand. He believes Hushai to be one of his supporters. Ahithophel, your grandfather and one of my advisors has turned and now supports Absolom. Hushai's servant tells me that Absolom was instructed to take my concubines which we left behind to watch the house. This is treason! It is as if to raise Absolom as king and publicly insult me. He has instructed Absolom to come seek us out here in our refuge and slay me to ensure the kingdom."

"Gracious!" Bathsheba exclaimed. "Is this what is happening? Are there riders headed our way? Why would my grandfather do such a thing?" David pulled another bite of bread off the loaf and shook his head.

"In continuing his deceit with Absolom, Hushai gave opposite counsel. He affirmed that although I am distant, my military reputation speaks for itself. That I am still his father, a formidable opposition like a bear protecting her cubs. My men are competent, experienced soldiers. Surrender is not why we fled and we will fight!"

Suddenly a stone hit the table from outside the tent. There was a man outside cursing profusely. David rose and stepped outside.

"You worthless man of blood! This is the Lord's vengeance on you for shaming the house of Saul!" The man threw a few more stones at David and a crowd had gathered to watch as this man confronted David.

"Sire, let me take off this man's head! How dare he curse you! Perhaps he is with Absolom!" A man from the crowd bravely stepped forward to confront the cursing man. David raised his hand to silence him as Bathsheba continued to cower near the tent's entrance.

"Why silence him? If the Lord indeed as instructed him to do so, I welcome the rebuke. My own son seeks my life, why should I fear this man too? Leave him alone." David turned to the crowd gathered.

"Let us pack up and continue to the Jordan." He looked at the cursing man with a resigned glance as he turned back into his tent to begin packing. Bathsheba watched him for a moment before asking, "Why do we continue to wander? If Adonai is to be with us like you say, then why not face Absolom?"

David stopped in his packing and turned to face Bathsheba. "I have learned that there are times to fight, and times to flee. I am once again waiting on the timing of God Almighty. To wait and face Absolom before I have heard to do so by God Himself would be disobedience on my part. There have been times in my life when I have had to hide in caves when Michal's father, King Saul sought to kill me in his jealousy, but my time to be king had not yet come. I had many opportunity to kill Saul myself, but I know not to lay a hand on God's anointed. I even feigned being mad in my fear of being killed. What a weak man I am!"

Bathsheba watched her husband's face contort in a mixture of grief for his sons whom had twisted into men of hate and fear over what to do to protect his life and those of his household.

"I know Adonai is with me and will provide a way. But how I struggle with His discipline for me. Nathan told us that the sword would not depart from our house. My sin brought this strife on us and I fear that sometimes it will be more than I can bear."

"I am here, husband." Bathsheba said meekly, her words falling flat to her own ears. David smiled. "I am cheered by your company, but in times like this I miss Jonathan. His friendship was so dear to me is often surpasses the love of a woman."

"Jonathan?"

"Michal's brother, Saul's son. We were closer than brothers. He helped save my life when Saul wanted me dead but was killed on the battlefield. My heart has never fully recovered from the loss of him."

Bathsheba silently turned and began gathering her own things in preparation to move. Abigail appeared at the tent's entrance, holding the hand of Solomon. "He was asking for you."

Bathsheba paused and let her son run into her open arms. David too wrapped his arms around them both.

"Adonai has blessed me with many good wives and children. I will not let my sadness with Absolom consume me." Abigail moved out of the way as a messenger ran to the tent's entrance.

"Sire, I have received word about your advisor Ahithophel back in Jerusalem." David turned from Bathsheba and Solomon to face the messenger.

"Yes? What have you heard?"

"Ahithophel now stands with Absolom and counseled your son to lie with the concubines you left at the palace to run the household in your absence. In doing so, Absolom is showing his intent of usurpation of your throne. Ahithophel was not permitted by Absolom to pursue you however as he wished to and in his grief has hung himself. His treason would have been discovered by you and had fallen out of favor with Absolom. An impossible situation."

"Thank you. That is all." David dismissed the messenger and Abigail immediately followed. Bathsheba held Solomon's hand and they watched David pace the tent.

"It would seem that Adonai is speaking after all. A confrontation between me and Absolom is looming sooner than later. I expect to see him when we cross the Jordan."

Bathsheba's heart leapt into her throat. Her grandfather, Ahithophel had committed treason against her husband. She silently prayed that God would be merciful.

CHAPTER TWENTY

A bird called from high in the treetop. Bathsheba followed Solomon's gaze upward as they tried to spot the foul among the leaf laden branches. They had been camped outside the forest in the land of the tribe of Ephraim, north of Jerusalem. Solomon clapped as he spotted the bird as it took to flight. Bathsheba smiled.

"Ready for some lunch?" She asked her son and they turned back to camp. Hoofbeats could be heard and Bathsheba turned to look over her shoulder. David's soldiers were returning to camp after being gone a few days scouting for any word from Absolom. The tension was nerve-wracking. His revolt against David was palatable and everyone wondered when the fighting would begin.

"Let's hurry." Bathsheba coaxed Solomon to join her in running back to camp in the dust of the returning scouts. She joined a crowd that was gathering in the center of camp where David stood waiting to hear from the messengers as they dismounted off their horses.

"Absolom's men have been spotted five miles east of here. They are preparing for battle and we should not wait to be ambushed."

David nodded at the report a previous look of resolve on his face. Bathsheba held Solomon's shoulders as her mouth ran dry. Solomon looked up at his mother. "What's happening?"

Bathsheba just patted his shoulders, not trusting her voice to be able to speak at the moment. The time for battle had come.

"Whatever seems the best strategy I will do. But I order you to deal gently for my sake with Absolom." David instructed his commanders and sent the army forth. Bathsheba stood with the other women and children in the camp and watched as the troops formed, dressed in their battle gear and weaponry and rode off to meet Absolom's men. The hoofbeats thundering as they rode past to the horizon.

"Mama, I'm still hungry." Young Solomon pleaded when they had departed. Smiling, Bathsheba welcomed the distraction. She took one more look to the warriors that were growing small in her vision and turned to her son.

CHAPTER TWENTY ONE

Joab rode with the men he commanded with determination. The words of the king's commandment rang in his unbelieving ears. *'Deal gently for my sake with Absolom.'*

It was difficult to swallow. Here they were in the wilderness of Ephraim when they should be safely in Jerusalem where David had earned the right to reign as King. Hadn't Jehovah himself anointed the son of Jesse? Instead they were allowing that spoiled brat Absolom dictate this civil unrest. Joab was going into battle. This was a position he was very familiar and comfortable with. He had served with his king for many years and established himself as a reliable advisor and leader among the King's Mighty Men. He feared in this instance however, that the king's ability to be objective was greatly compromised. Had this been any other enemy, Joab believed David would have acted swiftly and with little mercy. He remembered full well when David had sent Uriah to the front of the fighting knowing he would be killed. Joab was uneasy at the commands of his king as of late and wondered if they were as self serving as they had been back then.

A rider came up to them and matched their horses speed. "Commander!"

Joab raised his arm in a fist to signal his men to pause as he pulled back on his own reins to slow his steed. The horse stomped impatiently under him as he asked the reason for the interruption.

"Sir, Absolom has been spotted on a donkey riding within the oaks nearby. If you turn and follow me, we can ambush him now."

Excitedly, Joab nodded in agreement and called to his commanders behind him to pass the word. They were intercepting with Absolom, be ready. He clicked his heels into the belly of his horse and sped off after the scout in the direction where he last saw Absolom. After a bit, Joab caught sight of him on the donkey trying to outrun the troops of David that were gaining on him. Joab raised his arm and let out a battle shout which was the sign for his men to pursue and engage the intended enemy. They fanned out to surround Absolom which he perceived and instructed his men to do the same and meet the opposition. Arrows began to fly the fighting began. Joab stubbornly followed Absolom who had turned sharply left where the trees drew dense, trying to be harder to spot. Joab followed just outside the tree line, closing the distance between him and David's son.

Suddenly Absolom screamed as his donkey continued with forward momentum, and he lurched violently backward out of the saddle and left hanging in a low tree branch that was now tangled in the prince's long, thick hair. Joab smiled sadistically at the spectacle and continued to ride toward the scene. One of his men arrived at Absolom first but after he dismounted, just looked up at Absolom hanging there, kicking violently and did nothing.

"*Kill him!*" Joab screamed. "What is the *matter* with you?" Within seconds, he too was at the tree and flew off his horse before it had stopped running. Absolom continued to kick at them in rebellious defiance. With a furious shove, Joab screamed at his subordinate, "Why did you not pull Absolom out of the tree? I would have paid thee ten pieces of silver for such a valiant act!" The warrior sprawled in the dust at Joab's shove. Joab turned and tried to pull Absolom out of tree himself, dodging and ducking the kicks. The soldier on the ground picked himself up, began to plead with Joab who was blind with rage as Absolom continued to flail on the tree branch like a piece of fruit dancing in the wind.

"Sir, I would not put forth my hand against the king's son for you heard David command us to deal gently with him."

Absolom began to sneer from the tree. "Weasel of a man! Listening to that sniveling monarch! You fool!" This angered Joab all the more.

"I will not waste time like this! I will show you how to deal with this man!" He quickly pulled out some darts from within the sheaf in his belt and threw them at Absolom. The prince screamed as one of the darts hit him in the chest.

More of David's men had gathered under the oak tree, alerted by the noise of the commotion. Ten men together pulled at Absolom's legs and ripped him from the tree. Absolom fell to the ground with thud as the armor-bearers surrounded him like a pack of hungry wolves. They repeatedly struck him with fists, stones and daggers until he was dead. Joab triumphantly blew a trumpet to signal the troops to retreat. They had slain the rebellious leader and further battle would not be necessary. He tied Absolom as he would a wayward sheep from a herd and remounted his horse, dragging Absolom's body to a clearing among the oak trees. The applause and victorious shouting from his men was deafening.

More thuds and screams could be heard nearby. Joab's platoon turned toward the sound and discerned it was Absolom's men fleeing and they too were being toppled off their mounts by craggy low hanging tree branches.

"The trees shall fall them!"

"Jehovah has employed the aid of the might oaks to help us win the victory!"

"What a humiliating end to one who was so proud!"

The men shouted and cheered. They dumped Absolom's body unceremoniously in a pit they had dug and threw stones on it, building a pile. Cheering and celebrating, they mounted their horses and chased Absolom's troops to retreat.

Joab stood, breathing hard as the surge of adrenaline stopped coursing through his veins. He took in the haphazard pile of stones over the body of Absolom that a few flies had begun to scope out. The stench of death was alluring in battle victory and Joab took a large whiff into his nostrils.

"Mighty warrior." Joab spat sarcastically. "You dared to take the throne of God's anointed, King David? May this monument be in remembrance of your fall from grace, you worthless dog."

The timid servant known as a Cushite stood nearby and had been watching Joab a few paces away. "Shall I bring word to the king that his enemies have fallen?" He asked his commander meekly. Joan turned to him and replied. "No. We will tell the king tomorrow for today we mourn as a nation the death of the king's son." His words seemed hollow in his own ears. It was in respect for his king that he was erring to the side of reverence for Absolom's death. He felt no shame or sadness. The execution was justifiable. Necessary. David's love for his son had clouded his ability to recognize the danger of a divided kingdom. Absolom's propaganda was trouble, coupled with an ego that wouldn't quit.

"Go tell the king all you have seen." Wearily, Joab instructed the servant. The man bowed in respect and ran off. Another warrior who stood nearby cried out, "Are you kidding? This is a great day! Let me out-run that whimp and inform the king of our victory!"

Joab turned to the man. There was no victory. This entire situation had been tragic and its end brought no more reason. "There is no reward for you to bring the news to the king instead of that man from Cush."

The soldier shrugged cockily, "Sir?"

Joab sighed. "If you want to run, then run." He watched the man dart off after the servant and wondered who would arrive to David first to tell him his son was dead. As he rode back to camp, he caught word that David had indeed been told and was weeping and mourning for his son, Absolom. A new wave of frustration hit Joab and he rode to David's tent.

Joab came to David who had covered his face wailing, "Oh, Absolom, how I wish I had died instead of you, my son! Oh, Absolom!"

Joab flew off his horse without securely tying it to a tree. "Was our effort in vain?" He began shouting at King David, forgetting all manner of etiquette. "If Absalom still lived he would have killed all of us who love and serve you well and I bet you'd be happy then! You are never happy! It as if you love your enemies and hate your friends! I risked my *life* for you, oh king! How is it you still mourn for this ungrateful worm that happened to share your blood! He wanted your throne, don't you get *that*? I swear to the Lord our God if you continue in this mourning, there will not be a man left supporting you for we shall all flee leaving you to face a worse fate of evil alone!"

David stopped weeping and looked at his trusted commander. He was right. It was not time for mourning, for Absolom had brought this on himself. Jehovah had once again proclaimed that David was His anointed. David was more devastated by his own sin that had brought such distraction on his own household and was humbled that God saw fit to still use such a man as himself.

Joab quieted himself and spoke again, this time employing respect for the dignitary before him. "Sir, I beg your pardon. We have fought bravely against this threat to your kingdom. It is a pity that it also happens to be your son. I have served you faithfully all these years, followed your commands, trusted in Jehovah. Absolom had to be stopped. My lord, you *know* that."

"Thank you for your bold honesty with me." David told Joab as he rose from the floor. "You are right. I spent too much time grieving a son who was lost to me a long time ago." He turned to resume his position at the tent of meeting to hear civil cases but as he left he instructed Joab, "Spread the word, we return to the palace in Jerusalem first thing in the morning."

Joab smiled and bowed to his king. The man of God he knew and served had returned.

CHAPTER TWENTY TWO

Bathsheba awoke when a ray of light slipped through the tent cloths. She squinted and rolled away from the light. Sitting up and stretching, she looked sleepily about the room. Today she needed to pack up for they were leaving for home. Jerusalem. How she had missed it. She heard the scratch of a quill on papyrus and turned to see David scribbling in a corner. She had missed his presence in recent nights. Living as one of his wives, he spread his time with all of them. Out here in the wilderness, away from home, Bathsheba had felt loneliness, even when Solomon was her constant companion. David had chosen to stay with her last night.

"What is on your mind so early this morning?"

David turned to look at her and smiled. "Good morning, sleepyhead." He waved at the tent door. "The bleating from the kids in the herd awoke me with the sun. God gave me a new song and I am trying to write it down before I forget it."

"You were inspired by the recent battle?"

David's look left the tent and he visited a place deep within his mind. Bathsheba marveled at how quickly the sparkle could leave his eyes.

"Two of my sons have died. Amnon and Absolom are resting with our fathers because of my sin." Bathsheba had moved to stand behind David at his writing table. He took her hand in his and looked into her eyes. The sparkle in his eyes had returned.

"Actually, three of my sons have died if you count the young baby God took so quickly from us when I first brought you here as my wife. Sin has devastating consequences and God's mercy in spite of myself is overwhelming. I need to make sure that future generations don't forget this. Israel needs to keep God's ways in their minds and to follow His statutes as He commanded."

Bathsheba smiled. "God has chosen such a godly man to lead His nation." David smiled weakly at the compliment. "I feel more like an indentured servant to Him, Jehovah has given us so much."

Can I hear some of the song you have written?" Bathsheba asked.

David began to read:

" I love you, O, Lord my strength.
The Lord is my rock, my fortress and my deliverer.
My stronghold and my refuge.
My savior, Thou saves me from violence.
I will call upon the Lord.
Who is worthy to be praised.
I am saved from my enemies.
For the waves of death encompassed me
and confronted me.
In my distress I called upon the Lord
and my cry came to His ears.
Mine enemy was too mighty for me,
but the Lord was my stay. He delivered me, because
He delighted in me."

David's voice caught in his throat and his eyes swelled with tears. "How can he delight in me, wife? I have utterly disappointed him so. There is no good within me. Why would God call me?"

Bathsheba bent to throw her arms around his shoulders. "It is as your song reads, husband. He is our rock. Our Deliverer and Refuge. His ways are higher than ours. Who is greater than Jehovah? Israel exists to show the world of His Sovereignty."

David answered her, nodding. "His ordinances are before me and from his statures I will not turn aside. The Lord is with the humble people but Thy eyes are upon the haughty to bring them down. His way is perfect, the promise of the Lord proves true."

David stood and opened the tent. The sun was peering over the horizon and Bathsheba shivered a bit at the morning chill. "Today we return to mighty Jerusalem."

Soon they were on their way. Horses and donkeys laden with riders and goods, followed by livestock and people walking, the royal procession made their way south back to the capitol of Israel. The people who had stayed behind had lined the streets and were waving strips of cloth joyously. David smiled as the parade slowly made their way inside the city walls. The crowd parted and a young man stood waiting, propped up by two crudely fashioned crutches. His smile was as crooked as his legs as he welcomed King David. His beard had not trimmed and his clothes were dirty and dusty like that of a beggar. When the two locked eyes, David called to halt. He stepped out of his chariot and greeted him with a warm hug.

"Mephibosheth!"

Bathsheba watched from her seat on a the back of a donkey and her brow furrowed. Michal who was riding near her nodded toward the young man on crutches.

"That is my brother Jonathan's son, my nephew. David loves and cares for him out of respect for Jonathan."

"That is Saul's grandson?" Bathsheba asked.

"Yes." Michal replied defensively. "And my nephew."

"He cannot walk?"

"It is a tragic story. When word reached the palace that my brother and father had been killed on the battlefield during the siege of Jezreel, Mephibosheth was only a child of five. His nurse had been fleeing and carrying him, but in her haste, tripped. He fell to the ground and broke both legs. They never healed properly."

"May the Lord be merciful!"

"It is David who has shown the mercy to the lad."

"Why have I never seen him before now?" Bathsheba couldn't take her eyes off David and how he was dotting over the adolescent.

"Mephibosheth has been living with Ziba, a servant of Saul's, provided by David's generosity."

Bathsheba looked back at Michal, hearing a change in the tone of her voice. "You do not approve?"

"It is not that I resent David from being generous to Jonathan's son, for it honors his memory greatly. It is Ziba I do not trust. There has been word that he has taken David's spoils for his own enjoyment and not tended to Mephibosheth as he should."

"Does David know?"

Michal shook her head, her earring clinking from the lobes. "It does not appear so."

"I waited for your return!" Miphibosheth cried to David when he was released from the embrace. "I know you would come back to us someday."

"Why did you not join us, dear Miphibesheth?" David asked.

"Travel is difficult for me, as you can imagine. I told my servant to saddle up my donkey, for my heart longed to be with you. But he deceived me and I was not permitted to go."

"Zila shall divide my spoils and I will ensure you are cared for better."

"You are safely home, King David. What else do I need? Zila can have it all. I bear no hard feelings toward him."

David chuckled with laughter and swooped Miphibosheth up in his strong arms and carried him to a nearby donkey. Bathsheba moved her animal a bit to make room for him and took the crutches from a servant. She exchanged a smile with him.

"My son!" Miphibosheth called. David turned to see a servant holding an infant in her arms.

"Your son can come too!" David pronounced. The servant passed the child to Michal's empty arms. The procession started moving again toward the royal palace.

It was good to be back in familiar surroundings. Bathsheba stood at her window overlooking the city with Solomon that evening. Together they watched the sun color the sky with shades of pink and orange.

"Did you see that man today mother? The one father picked up and put in the carriage?"

"Indeed, I did, Solomon. He is the son of a dear friend and your father cares for him."

"What is his name?"

"They call him Miphibesheth."

"Meffff . . . . . Meffibbbb . . . that is hard to say."

Bathsheba softly chuckled. "It is quite a name. It means 'out of my mouth proceeds correction.'"

"What does that mean?"

"I suppose it is the parent righting the ways of the child as Jehovah does for Israel, or how I used to correct you when you were younger, Solomon." Bathsheba turned to tickle him playfully. He giggled and squirmed.

"What does my name mean?"

Bathsheba turned to look him in the eye. "Solomon is taken from our word Shalom. It means peace."

"Peace. Does that mean I am to be a man in the courts someday?"

Bathsheba looked in her son's eyes, searching for an answer. In her heart, she wanted great things for her son. She dreamed of him becoming an important man, God-fearing like his father. She had no words and in her silence, Solomon's mind clicked to another thought.

"I saw the crowds as we entered Jerusalem, but the city seems smaller somehow, doesn't it mother?"

"How keen is your observations my son. Yes, some of Israel is still loyal to Absolom, your half-brother. Even in death, his politics still rumble within some hearts that are disloyal to your father, King David."

"Will there be more trouble?"

Bathsheba kissed her son on the cheek, begging her own fears not to surface from deep within her. "I hope not, my son. I hope not."

CHAPTER TWENTY THREE

Joab's feet echoed as he made haste to the king's court where he had been summoned. They had returned to Jerusalem a few weeks ago but the Mighty Men were still on alert for any word of revolt. He nodded to the two sentinels that stood outside David's door. He outranked them but it was important to still show honor to fellow soldiers. When he had closed the door behind him, he cleared his throat to announce his presence. David was staring out a window.

"Joab, thank you for coming." David turned and took a seat on an opulent chair and motioned for Joab to sit opposite him. There was a small fire burning in between them with a plate of figs and roasted lamb.

"Hungry?" One of the servants standing nearby moved closer with a pitcher of water. "Thirsty?"

Joab held up his hand. "No thank you, Sir."

David rubbed his hands together. "I have heard rumors since our return. What do you know about Amasa?"

"Appointed captain over the army by Absolom? Only that he still supposes that he holds that title, although that position is mine. You appointed me for that position, sir."

"Yes, I hear that he is unhappy with the news of Absolom's death and as you mentioned has illusions about his true position in our ranks. Is he trouble?"

Joab's loyalty to King David stood firm as it had for decades. "I am suspicious of anyone who does not recognize you as God's anointed. He seems to view me as a personal rival and has no qualms about taking lives of any who stand in his way. It does not sit well with me when anyone seems to want my job."

David nodded and stood. "That is what I have surmised as well. Take some men with you and pursue him. We need to stop him before he rallies up himself an army and leads a revolution in vengeance for Absolom. I do not trust my concubines whom I left to care for the house while we were absent. Please set them up in their own housing with a guard twenty-four hours a day lest they pass information to our enemies as well. Find Amasa and bring him to me so that I may question his motives."

Joab stood and bowed to David. "As you wish, my king. We will leave in the morning." David nodded and turned back to his window. Joab left the room, he paused a moment at the door and wondered if the king suspected that he had supported Abjoniah instead of David.

Joab assembled his men and explained the mission. They set out at first light, wearing battle garments once again. They headed to Gibeon where intel had notified them that Amasa had joined ranks with a Benjaminite named Sheba. Joab had been told that Sheba had shamelessly told anyone who would listen that he had no portion in David and was thus considered a threat to the kingdom. Joab set his jaw in frustration. Amasa was his cousin, but he too was guilty of treason and the mission was to stop him and his men in the name of King David and the protection of a unified Israel nation. Word had reached Amasa that Joab was riding out and the two met each other at a resting spot near a large stone in the desert, just outside the city of Gibeon.

The two men glared at each other, surrounded by their armies tense with impending conflict. "You did not attend a meeting when we summoned Judah." Joab began accusingly.

Amasa smiled smugly. "I don't answer to you or any of David's men. So you summoned me. I meet with men when I purpose to meet with men."

"Is it well with you?" Joab asked him.

Amasa chuckled and looked back at his men behind him as if to say, 'can you believe this guy?' He was so caught off guard by Joab's seemingly cordial tone, that he did not see Joab close the gap between them and grasp a sword in his hand.

"I am very well, now that I am free from that tyrant you call king!" Amana answered. Joab nodded and leaned in to Amasa who thought him to be greeting him with a kiss which has a customary sign of respect. Instead he roughly grabbed Amasa's beard in his left hand, gritting his teeth.

"My king is the anointed one of Israel. God himself has put David in position and you will not dishonor him!" Joab growled. He and Amasa were nose to nose. The men surrounding them saw the discourse and began grunting and exchanging insults among themselves. In one swift motion, Joab shouted at Amasa and drew the sword he had in his hand and shoved it full long into Amasa's torso.

Amasa screamed in pain and arched his back. His men saw the attack and ran toward Joab's men who met them with swords drawn. Another battle erupted. Joab continued to hold Amasa's shoulder with one hand and the handle of his sword with the other. When he felt the resistance of his blade from impaling Amasa, he grit his teeth and twisted the blade to the right and violently pulled the sword out.

Amasa's knees buckled and he fell to the ground, writhing in agony as his intestines began to spill from the wound. Joab stood over him and watched him until he breathed his last. His fingers clenched on the sword, ready to strike a second blow if necessary. He looked around and saw his men had gained the upper hand, far better trained than the rebellious crew of Amasa.

"Find Sheba!" Joab commanded and his men fanned out to retrieve the traitor. "Listen those who are here with Amasa. See your fallen leader. Do not follow this folly any longer, Sheba's demise will swiftly follow this one. If you intend to follow King David, get thee back to Jerusalem. If you are with David, then you are with me, for my loyalty will always be to him."

Breathing hard from the execution, Joab wiped his mouth with the back of the hand still grasping the sword and ran off in the direction of his men in search of Sheba. He found his men speaking to a woman who told them where she had seen Sheba within the walls of the city of Gibeon. One of his commanders ran up to Joab.

"Sir, she saw Sheba and has told us where he is hiding."

Joab nodded to his men who continued to run in their pursuit of Sheba and turned to the woman and thanked her. "You have wisdom like Deborah. I am not interested in more bloodshed, you have saved your city by pointing out the defector. I wish to release all peaceable inhabitants from further harm."

"May the head of Sheba be thrown against the city wall!" the woman exclaimed. Joab smiled and instructed her to spread the word. No sooner had she hobbled off when his men returned holding the head of Sheba by the hair as the woman had prophecied. They shouted with victory. Joab blew the trumpet indicating that the mission was successfully completed and it was time to return to Jerusalem. He had a report to deliver to King David.

Joab felt as though he was going through the motions. Fueled by his own internal struggle of where his loyalties truly lay, he felt angry and powerful. He was thankful for missions where he could expel some rage on those who were considered threats to the throne. Purging the kingdom of Absolom's insurrection was a thankless, tiresome chore. But when reporting back to King David, he felt his own ambiguity in the king. 'God's appointed' sure had a legacy of destruction and deceit. Could Joab truly trust in him?

King David had been frustratingly short with Joab. He had expected more gratitude and accolades from one he had so faithfully served so long.

Wearily wanting to put the whole messy situation behind him, David had Saul and Jonathan's bones and put them in a tomb with their ancestors. He had spared Mephibosheth, in honor of his friendship with Jonathan. Looking toward the heavens, David poured a heart of thanksgiving out to his God. Joan clasped his hands and decided to bide his time as he listened to David's prayer.

> "Shout for joy to the Lord, all the earth.
> Worship the Lord with gladness.
> Come before Him with joyful songs.
> Know that the Lord is god.
> It is He who made us and we are His.
> We are His people, the sheep of His pasture.
> Enter His gates with thanksgiving
> and His courts with praise;
> Give thanks to Him and praise His name.
> For the Lord is good and His love endures forever.
> His faithfulness continues through all generations."
> (Psalm 100)

CHAPTER TWENTY FOUR

Bathsheba's steps had slowed and her back arched a bit in her shuffled walk. She could feel the years on her body and read the tiredness of David's soul on his aging face. The handsome countenance was framed with silver hair for the years had passed swiftly. There was a woman named Abishag who had moved into the royal residence. She was a Shunamite and was instructed to keep King David warm at night. In his aging frailty, he shivered at the slightest breeze and his leathered hands always felt ice cold. Bathsheba took comfort that this woman was used not in a position of wife, but more medicinal in aiding David's surmounting geriatric needs. David no longer visited her chambers, or any other wife for that matter.

Rumors began to fly around Jerusalem as to who would succeed King David on his throne. There were many wives and children to speak of. With Amnon and Absolom slain, Adonijah, Haggish's son began to assume that he was the eldest son and proclaimed himself king. Like proud Absolom before him, he assumed position in the court and began making judgements and pronouncements before the honor had been officially bestowed upon him. This worried Bathsheba and she prayed for direction. Would God not appoint another king?

She decided to take matter into her own hands and called for audience with Nathan, the prophet. He had been diligently chronicling the life of David, his many battle victories and psalms. God had instructed Nathan to convict David's heart with this adulterous sin with her and Bathsheba knew that God's wisdom was still with Nathan. She met him in the garden.

"Thank you for allowing me some time to speak with you." Bathsheba replied.

"It is always good to speak with one of David's wives. He is a man after God's own heart."

"Why do you call him so?"

"David has many faults and has not lived a blameless life. But unlike his predecessor, King Saul, David does not seek his own way, but wishes to honor the will of God, even to the detriment of his own character. Oftentimes he has been transparent in his faults in front of his subjects. This is pleasing to Jehovah and He will bless David at all he puts his hand to. David wished to build for God a temple and has begun to gather the materials from the people and employed the architects to began drawing up plans for a permanent residence for the Ark of the Covenant. But that task is to be for his son. David's son will build the temple."

"Will there be another ruler that can follow David with such righteous spirit that you speak of? One that longs to build a temple for the glory of God?" Bathsheba inquired.

"Have you not heard that Adonijah, son of Haggish has proudly declared himself king? Who appointed him so? I do not see that he fears the Lord. However, one bold enough to put up airs for himself will easily be jealous and suspicious of those who can take it away."

"Of course. We are all aware that Adonijah is acting as king in David's convalescence and is waiting to receive the official blessing from him. What do you mean that Adonijah is suspicious?"

"King David has many wives and other children. Any one of these could give Adonijah cause to lose his throne. This may give him reason to have murderous intent. Listen to my counsel so that you and your son may live."

"I am listening."

"Go at once to King David and make him to swear that he will make Solomon king after his death."

"But David will only see me as a mother trying to give the best opportunity for my son. He will not heed my plea!" Bathsheba exclaimed.

"Indeed, while you are speaking with David, I will enter the room and confirm your request as from the Lord. I believe that Solomon is whom God is anointing after David lies with his fathers. I have watched your son. He has an inquisitive mind that sees details. He harbors no pride and would make a just ruler for Israel."

Bathsheba bowed to the man of God. "Thank you, Nathan. I will purify myself tonight in preparation for audience with the king."

Bathsheba arose the next morning nervous. She had spent a restless night watching the stars out her window from her bed. Sleep had eluded her and she passed the hours in prayer to Jehovah. He had saved her in the past, turned David's heart, blessed them with a strong son. Would now see fit to elevate Solomon to kingship over Israel?

David had agreed to see her and the two of them often spoke freely. She had been present during many of the writings of his songs, heard his heart during the dark days of trial and celebrated at his side with him at his victories. This conversation would be different however. She had settled into life within the kingdom walls as one of the wives. Abigail, Ma'acah, Haggith, Abital and Eglah. These women had been with Bathsheba all these years. They each had a position for leverage, perhaps some had already requested audience with David as she was doing on behalf of their own children. 'Adoni, give me strength!' she cried silently.

"Good morning wife." David greeted her pleasantly. "Would you care for some fresh honey cakes? They are still warm from the oven." He was sitting in his chair, leaning on one elbow. The years had taken their toll. He was shaking, unable to control his limbs and his speech was fragmented and slow. Bathsheba noticed Abishag sitting nearby, ever ready to do the king's biding. She kept her eyes low.

Bathsheba's heart was turning sommersaults. She held up her hand to politely refuse. She licked her lips, but her mouth was dry. She went to a pitcher that was nearby and gulped a goblet of water.

"Thank you for seeing me."

"What do you need?"

"My lord, you swore to your maidservant by the Lord our God saying that Solomon, our son should reign after you and sit on your throne. But Adonijah, Haggith's son, has already presented himself in court as king. The subjects are beginning to recognize his reign even though you have not esteemed him so. He has sacrificed many animals on the altar and invited audience with neighboring dignitaries and Joab, commander of the guard."

David grunted. "I was not aware of Adonijah's assumption. I am not yet in the grave and have made no such announcement."

"Yes, your lord." Bathsheba pressed on bravely, wondering when Nathan would appear in the room. "The entire population of Israel is waiting to hear your pronouncement of who shall sit on your throne. You are advanced in years and God has blessed you with warmth at night. Please speak soon of your desire for Solomon for the throne, or Adonijah will have the kingdom by default. I fear my safety and for Solomon's welfare lest Adonijah see us as traitors and threats to his kingdom."

As she finished speaking, she heard the door close. Nathan stood in the doorway. David's poor eyesight had not revealed to him who had entered, so a servant nearby informed him, "Nathan the prophet is here."

Nathan came before David and bowed reverently before him. He made eye contact with Bathsheba and nodded.

"Nathan, my trusted advisor with the wisdom of our Lord. Bathsheba was here calling out for the coronation of Solomon. What do you think?"

"My lord the king, have you ever called Adonijah as successor to your throne?" Nathan answered, taking a rational approach. "Where then would he get this idea? From his own pride that shadows that of his brother, Absolom. And where did Absolom's pride take him? Into sleep with the fathers. It is true what Bathsheba has told you. Adonijah by his own deduction has sacrificed with the priest as ruler of the land, instructed Joab as to where and when your army would move and begun negotiations with neighboring rulers as if he already was given the throne of Israel!"

"The danger lies with many people in the city already toasting and proclaiming 'long live King Adonijah' but there has been no indication from you, their true anointed leader, King David. Adonijah has not included the high priest, your wives or any other children into his pageantry and this shows me a heart filled with ambition and deceit. The time has come for you to speak publicly on this manner and answer all speculation once and for all."

David nodded. "Is Bathsheba still here?"

"I am, my lord." Bathsheba stepped out from behind Nathan and faced her husband.

"I swear this day, as the Lord lives who has redeemed my soul, It is Solomon, my son with Bathsheba whom shall sit upon my throne in my stead." David proclaimed. He called to his servants to call his royal scribes to hear the same pronouncement to that word could be spread throughout the land that David's choice was God's choice. Solomon was to be king.

Bathsheba bowed low with her face to the ground. "Long live King David, thank you, oh, thank you."

David felt around for her head and stroked her hair when he found it. "My dear Bathsheba, God has found our son worthy to carry on and reign Israel. Nathan, call the high priest Zadok and make preparations for Solomon to ride into the city presented as my choice for successor to the throne. Sound the trumpets and let the people say 'long live, King Solomon!'"

Nathan smiled at Bathsheba. "As you wish, my lord."

Days later, Bathsheba stood proudly in the assembly where David had heard many court cases and reigned in majesty. She watched as Solomon rode in on a donkey, led by Nathan who was blowing on the Shofar horn.

"Long live, King Solomon!" the people were shouting. Bathsheba looked around the room and took in the admiring eyes. God had done it again. Secured a position for her son and blessed them abundantly. Zadok the priest took out a horn of oil and poured it on Solomon's forehead, appointing him ruler over Israel and over Judah. Solomon looked so regal bowing in front of the priest. Bathsheba noticed the strong arms of her son and his flowing hair on his broad shoulders. Her boy was now a man. She smiled at the blessing he had been to her all these years. There was great celebration and feasting. David himself must have heard the jubilation from his bed in chambers for the pronouncement of his son Solomon as king.

Bathsheba saw Adonijah come forward, followed by Joab, the commander of the guard. She nervously looked over at Nathan whose face didn't betray any worry at all. Adonijah bowed before Solomon and conceded that David had chosen him as king over himself.

"I am fearful of you, brother. I have sacrificed on the altar with prayers that you would not have me killed."

Solomon, in his first act as reigning king replied to Adonijah.

"If you prove yourself worthy, not one of your hairs will be harmed. If you are found to be wicked of heart, however, I will deal with you as my father, King Daivd did with anyone who tried to take his throne by force and you will rest with our brother Absolom."

Adonijah nodded. "Understood." Looking around sheepishly at his followers who had come to see how it would play out, he murmured "Long live King Solomon." Hearing this, Adonijah's followers fled, although none pursued them.

Bathsheba looked to the heavens and offered up a prayer of thanksgiving as she had seen King David do so many times before. A new chapter had begun.

CHAPTER TWENTY FIVE

―✝―

Solomon took to his role as ruler very easily. Bathsheba credited God for this. She was surprised when she saw Adonijah come to court asking for audience with Solomon. He had conceded to Solomon's position as David's chosen for the throne instead of himself, but here he was. Would he now put up resistance?

Adonijah bowed respectfully in front of Solomon who nodded.

"Greetings, brother. What is it that you need that causes you to come to court today?" Solomon's baritone voice sounded so much like David's.

"If it pleases you, my lord. I have taken notice of the young Abishag, called here from her hometown of Shunem in the land of the tribe of Issachar. She has served the king well in his final years, but is away from her family." Adonijah paused and looked around the room nervously.

"Yes, Abishag has been faithful in her service to our father." Solomon agreed.

"She is as I say, alone here in Jerusalem, and my heart goes out to her. Not as a father to a daughter, but I would ask that I be able to marry Abishag. I wish to be her husband and to take care of her after our father's passing."

Solomon's brow furrowed. "I will consider the matter. You are dismissed. I will send for you when I reach a decision."

Bathsheba watched Adonijah bow again and leave the court. She was touched by his tenderness toward Abishag and felt for her. She was a woman given to David without a thought about how she would feel. She related to coming to the royal residence feeling alone. Perhaps Adonijah's heart had changed and this would be a good idea. She slipped out of court unnoticed and went after Adonijah.

"Sir, I beg a word with you!" She called after him. Adonijah turned.

"Bathsheba, mother of Solomon." He bowed to her respectfully. "What does the new king's mother require of me?"

"I heard you in court just now, asking for Abishag's hand in marriage. Do you truly care for her?"

"It would please me greatly to have Abishag as my wife. I have been impressed with a woman who can leave her family and serve such a frail man so selflessly. It shows great character. Do you suppose . . ." he stepped toward Bathsheba but stopped himself. Bathsheba was completely moved by his graciousness. She smiled.

"What were you going to ask me?"

"If it is not too bold, I wondered if you had any sway with your son? I know I am not popular with him, or perhaps even with you, but my intentions are pure. I wish to marry sweet Abishag and provide for her all my days."

Bathsheba squinted as she eyed Adonijah. She tried to weigh his motives and search out if he indeed was being truthful.

"When King David sleeps with his fathers, where will that leave Abishag?" Adonijah continued. "She will be alone. No house to speak of, no means to return to her home in Shunem, no dowry to offer. Please! Ask Solomon to permit me to take Abishag as my wife."

"It is an honorable thing you ask, to take in a servant of King David's."

Adonijah bowed again to Bathsheba. "I would be honored if you spoke with Solomon on this matter."

Bathsheba nodded decisively. "I will speak with my son on your behalf." Adonijah smiled widely. "Oh, thank you so. Your humble servant is most grateful." He turned and walked away. Bathsheba watched him leave and turned to return to court. She snuck back in and sat down silently, immediately drawn into another conflict.

A woman was holding a crying child, weeping before Solomon.

"Sir, I beg you the child is mine!"

Another women was on her knees next to her, wailing so loudly it echoed off the limestone columns. "She's lying! The child she holds is not hers, it is mine!" The woman holding the child grasped it tighter and turned from the travailing woman on the floor who began to crawl after her. "Please, please . . . ."

Bathsheba shifted uncomfortably in her seat. Both women were in distress over who the child belonged to. She watched Solomon's eyes as he took in the scene. He held up his hand to silence the two women and guards moved in a few paces to encourage the women to obey.

"Woman," Solomon addressed the mother on the floor. "Rise and tell me your tale."

The woman drew herself to her feet and wiped her face with the hem of her robe. She nodded in respect to Solomon, and although she was still racked with heaving sobs, she began to speak.

"Sir, I share a home with this woman." She waved her hand to the crying woman holding the baby. "Our husbands have died and we bore children about the same time. Tragically, a few nights ago, while sleeping with her child, she accidentally smothered it and took my child, calling it her own. She claims that the dead boy is my son."

"She is a *liar!*" The other woman screamed. "I hold my son in my arms. It is she who smothered her child in her bed and in her grief was been spreading the lie that I traded the children! This is not true! Make her stop chasing me with her falsehoods!"

Solomon raised his hand to silence the women again and stood. He held a hand to his mouth, deep in thought and paced in front of his throne a bit. Bathsheba stood breathless, aching for the women. She knew the horrible cloud of grief that comes with losing a child. Certainly one of them did lose a child in death and the other is lying, but who is who? How would Solomon ever be able to determine the truth? Bathsheba prayed for God to show Solomon an answer.

Solomon called for the guards. "Truly both of these women love their child. It is impossible to determine which mother the baby belongs to. Give me your sword."

A gasp went out throughout the crowd as one of the guards dutifully withdrew the sword from its sheath on his side and gave it to Solomon.

"I will cut the baby in half. I shall give the top torso to you, and the waist and legs to you. It is a fair determination that each of you have half the child since the other child is dead."

The women holding the baby cried and kissed the child's head, holding him tighter. The woman standing with empty hands began to cry fresh tears, a look of horror on her face.

"No, sire!" She cried out. "Please, I beg of you, please do not kill the boy. She can have him." She indicated to the woman holding the baby. The woman holding the child hatefully spat at her "Foolish woman, did you not hear? Our just King has pronounced the child be split among us so that neither shall be able to serve as his mother!"

The woman without the child totally ignored the insult and addressed Solomon again.

"If she claims the child at least he will be cared for and live and I can die knowing my son was loved."

Solomon walked to the woman with the child and instructed her to give the baby to him. She did so and looked at the other women with disgust. The other woman stretched out her arms a bit and then let them fall limply at her side. She hung her head and began to cry, sobbing so violently, her shoulders moved as if being shook by an invisible hand. "Please don't kill him, please don't kill him." She whimpered. The other woman folded her arms in anger and watched Solomon with the child.

"A true mother is concerned with the well-being of her child. Did not Moses' mother place him in a basket to spare his life even if it meant never seeing him again? Did not Hannah promise to give her son Samuel back to God for his service if Jehovah opened her womb?" Solomon gently bounced the child and got it to stop crying. He walked over to the weeping woman.

"I know that you are the true mother, for you requested me to spare his life." He handed the baby to her and she cried out with a happy gasp. She embraced the child and kissed him.

"Oh, thank you, my lord, thank you!" She bowed and fled from the room.

Solomon strode over to the imposter who was still glaring at him with hateful eyes.

"That child was *mine!*"

Solomon went to her and faced her. She did not bow but defiantly stood facing him.

"Arrest this woman."

She cried out as the guards seized her. As they led her away, Solomon spoke to the room.

"May it be known in the kingdom that this woman shall be executed for her spiteful decision. It is tragic that her son was smothered by her in her sleep, but it was evil for her to kidnap another and spread a lie to make others think the child was her own. Worse yet, she would rather see that child die than to deal with her own grief. This will not be tolerated. Israel has no room for liars and murderers. We are God's chosen nation and are to live righteously unto Him."

Solomon's robe, hemmed in gold stitching flowed as he purposefully strode from the room. Bathsheba sat amazed at his wisdom and thanked God for providing it to her son when he needed it. The case of the two women spread through the kingdom like wildfire. It was known that Solomon was a just ruler, full of wisdom and he grew in popularity.

He had sent word to Bathsheba that he was willing to speak with her that evening. She immediately went to meet with him. He was sipping a goblet of wine and smiled when she entered the room.

"Mother!" He held her shoulders and kissed her cheek in greeting.

"You were a wonder to watch at court today. Those poor women!"

"Woman." Solomon corrected. "The other was deceitful and selfish."

Bathsheba shook her head. "It was awe inspiring how you discerned that!" Solomon sat on his throne and had a guard bring a chair for his mother to sit near him.

"God alone grants me wisdom. I have desired nothing else. It has been quite a long day. What brings you hear at this hour?"

"I spoke with Abonijah at court this afternoon after he petitioned you for permission to marry Abishag." Bathsheba replied. Solomon shifted in his chair. "I find his heart to be pure, Abonijah truly cares for Abishag and wishes that she was his wife. You are considering to grant permission, aren't you?"

"Mother, I will never refuse audience with you. You, like Abishag, have served my father King David with the highest respect and he has loved you for many years. Why do you ask me this for Abonijah? He is my eldest brother, why not ask for me to give him my kingdom as well?"

Bathsheba sat there dumbfounded. Why was he getting so agitated?

"As the Lord lives, it is He who established me here as king of Israel to follow in my father David's footsteps. Abonijah is not God's choice and will be put to death for his insubordination."

Bathsheba found her voice. "Insubordination? But Abonijah came to you today, conceding that you indeed are king, not him. He only asks for marriage, not your throne."

"Woman, you are mistaken." Solomon's tone became more firm. "In asking for Abishag in marriage, Abonijah is in fact trying to thwart my position as king and claim it as his own. Taking the wife or concubine of the father has been a sign of rebellion for generations!"

"But Abishag is not a wife! She simply warms your father during chilly nights."

"She shares his bed. She belongs to King David and in taking her, Abonijah is challenging my kingdom. When Absolom slept with father's concubines when we were away from Jerusalem, he was doing the same thing! Trying to take father's throne by force! Such arrogance will not be tolerated! Abonijah has already been sentenced to death. I have already commissioned Benaiah to carry out the execution in the morning. Furthermore, the priest Abiathar who assisted Abonijah when he gave sacrifices as a ruling power will be banished from the kingdom."

"No, my son . . ." Bathsheba tried to interject but Solomon interrupted her.

"It would bode you well to not press the matter further. I respect you mother, but as your king, I have made my decision." Solomon stood which gave the guards the signal to walk to Bathsheba to escort her from the room.

She swallowed hard. Solomon was her son, but tonight she saw a side of him not discerned before. She closed the door behind her as she left Solomon's presence and muffled a sob that threatened to escape her lips.

CHAPTER TWENTY SIX

David had asked to see Solomon. His breathing had become labored and he knew his time was near. He wanted to bestow the patriarchal blessing on his successor. David asked to be propped up in his bed so he might gaze out the window. He hadn't been out in the sunshine for months. He sat there motionless, remembering scenes from his life. The bravery he demonstrated to King Saul when he faced Goliath with his shepherd's sling. Faded deeper in the recesses of his mind were times as a boy on a hillside facing a roaring lion that was threatening the sheep. Somehow within him, he was absolutely fortified with the assurance that God would give him the victory on those occasions. He felt anew the shame of Uriah's murder after his lust for Bathsheba. He knew God forgave him years ago, but still squirmed at the realization of how evil his flesh was. He was so thankful to merciful Jehovah that from those ashes he blessed them with a loving marriage and a wise son, Solomon. Somehow, God still called David a godly leader and David prayed that his kingdom would prove to continue to have a reputation of righteousness for Israel.

"Good morning, father." Solomon entered the room and bowed deeply at his bedside. He brought a plate of food. "Can I offer you fruit or a piece of fish?"

David weakly shook his head. "No, food no longer sits well in my stomach. Come sit beside me." Solomon obeyed and held his father's hands in his.

"I am about to die, my son. I wanted to tell you to be strong. It is difficult to lead a stiff-necked people. Show yourself to be a man and keep God's commandments and ordinances before you as a beacon. It is only in doing this and following the Mosaic law that you may prosper in all you do. I have had occasion in my life when I have forgotten that and paid dearly."

"Sin has a price. Do not forget that you are never beyond it's grasp. Even as king you have a great responsibility to keep yourself from temptation lest your weakness cause the entire nation of Israel to stumble. Teach your children to do the same and to follow the Lord with all the faithfulness in their heart and souls."

"Yes, father. I desire to serve God humbly and if I could be half the man you were during your reign I will be happy." Solomon kissed his father's knobby hands.

"I need you to do something for me." David whispered, his voice growing weak. Solomon quietly poured a cup of water for his father and helped him drink.

"What do you request father? I will gladly do anything for you."

"Joab, my commander in the guard, has been my faithful companion since we were both very young men. He has been with me up until Absolom's treason, but most recently, he was assisting Adonijah in his claim to the throne. He stood against my choice as you, dear Solomon for kingship. Furthermore, he dealt with Amasa with cruel murderous intent instead of bringing him to me for questioning when there was talk of Amasa's own thoughts of treason. Joab avenged blood for his own purposes during a season of peace in Israel."

"I remember." Solomon replied.

"You must deal with this in your wisdom, my son. You know what you need to do. It was most grievous that Joab feigned to be coming to Amasa in friendship and instead met him with a sword. Let not his head go to his grave in peace either. I have been culpable to right this wrong for some time and have delayed it long enough. According to God's law, Joab should die for murder."

Solomon nodded. "I will see to it father, I swear to the Lord that your words will be carried out."

David smiled weakly and closed his eyes. "You are a good son. Follow God all your days. Follow God . . . . follow Him without fail . . . ."

Solomon watched as his father slipped away. The cold hands that he still held in his own went limp. Solomon immediately felt on David's throat for a pulse but could not find one. He gently placed David's hands across his chest and dropped his head, weeping.

Solomon rose and went to the window and looked over Jerusalem. The streets were busy with people buying spices, sacrifices, greeting each other, civil matters . . . life would now continue on without mighty King David.

"Aughhhhhhhh!" Solomon roared like a lion in grief for his father's death. He ripped his robe and fell to his knees. The weight of being king of Israel had never felt so heavy as it did in that moment.

CHAPTER TWENTY SEVEN

Solomon stood on the mountain overlooking the mighty city. It was still in mourning for it's great leader, King David as it had for the past month. Solomon himself had cut off his hair and beard which was just now beginning to grow back in brown stubble. The culmination of this grieving time ended today with Solomon's sacrifice to God. Solomon remembered all that his father, David had taught him. He had dutifully carried out Joab's execution as his father requested on his deathbed. Now the sacrifice was ready. The stones were on the altar, the fire was about to be offered, the ram bound nearby.

Solomon drew a large breath into his lungs and held it there for a moment. Searching his soul, he closed his eyes. Breathing out, he began to pray to God.

"I love you Lord and strive to walk in your statues as my father instructed me. I asked of you last night when you appeared to me in my dreams, oh God. I am yet but a boy. I do not know how to lead these people! I do not know how to go out or how to come in! You have shown great and steadfast love to David because he walked faithfully with you. I desire to do the same."

Solomon fell to his knees before the altar, hands clasped in earnest dialogue with Jehovah. "Give your servant an understanding mind to govern Your people. God, I ask for nothing than the ability to distinguish right from wrong. I love you

Lord of Abraham, Isaac and Jacob. I trust in you, oh God of my father, David. Consider your humble servant worthy to follow in such a legacy of righteousness."

"I thank you Lord that you responded to me in my dream. You promised me long life and riches, blessings I did not ask for but bestowed upon me because you delighted in my desire for your wisdom. I am humbled that no other king shall compare and will honor you by building you a temple in which to dwell. Please continue to be with your people, Israel. Make us a great nation upon the earth for your glory."

"You are our Provider, generous, merciful Lord. You are worthy of our praise." With his priests, Solomon offered the ram to God on the mountain near Gibeon. He walked down the hill a bit and met up with his men who had traveled with him for the sacrifice. They waited expectantly for his direction. Solomon still felt very inadequate, but clothed himself with the assurance that like his father David, God was with him. His request for wisdom was granted and he resolved to operate in that knowledge. He instructed his men as they walked back to Jerusalem.

"Let the word go forth that the season for mourning my father, great King David is over. We go forward as a new generation, serving and glorifying God in all of our ways as the mighty nation of Israel. Call the architects and have them begin drawing up plans to build the temple by father had begun. We need to give God a home to dwell in. Haven't we all places to reside? Our gracious Jehovah deserves the same."

"My father was a writer of psalms that we use in our worship. Make sure the scribes get them written down for history. Ask the advisors, my mother Bathsheba, and myself to recite the songs given to David through God. I have asked for wisdom in my reign from God Almighty and believe that he heard my prayer. I ask the scribes to meet with me regularly to write down information God provides me for the benefit of many. Proverbs, geology, anatomy, political and practicality. Our Creator does know this all full well and has permitted Him humble servant to be His voice during my reign. I shall not fail Him. King Saul ruled forty years, as did my father, King David. May God bless Israel as my chapter begins."

"You indeed are blessed with peace and prosperity, oh king." One of his advisors agreed. "The kingdom lacks nothing, we have plenty of provisions, herds and resources. Furthermore, Israel is experiencing a season of peace, no advisory is threatening us. What then shall we do?"

"The most important thing is to build God's temple." Solomon reiterated. "We will waste no time in constructing it. Command the cedars found in Lebanon to be cut for me. Set up wages for the servants. Have a census and tell me as soon as possible how many able bodies we have for the work. We shall begin."

All of Jerusalem celebrated when Solomon returned from his time of sacrifice. With mourning for King David complete, the nation set its sights on building the temple. In the next few months, construction was commencing. At the last count, there were over thirty thousand men at the working with piles of materials scattered everywhere. The years passed and Israel worked steadily. God continued to provide and bless the nation.

One day, Solomon sent for his mother, Bathsheba to show her the temple progress. Beautiful Bathsheba had aged into a small woman. Solomon in his manhood now towered over her. She walked haltingly now but still had her quiet sense about her. The gray hair curled around her brow and small wrinkles had worked their way into her porcelain skin. She held a swatch of fabric at her neck, to keep it in place covering her head. She met her son at the temple construction site.

"Thank you for coming, mother. It is important that I get your opinion on how we are progressing with building God's temple."

"It is marvelous! Much more elegant that I could imagine!" Bathsheba gushed. "Solomon, you have spared nothing!"

"God deserves the very best." Solomon stretched his arm out. "The temple is one hundred and eight feet long. If you were to take the height of the walls of Jerusalem and lay them on their side, it would take almost three of them to be the length of the temple."

Solomon chuckled at Bathsheba's gasp. "I have chosen to use Cedar aromatic cedar trees brought in from Lebanon, the best limestone from the quarries — untouched by tools here on the construction site so they are so smooth. Come feel." Bathsheba rubbed her hand over one of the white squares and marveled that she barely felt any dust under her fingertips.

"This must be costing you a fortune!" Bathsheba exclaimed. Solomon shrugged. "God deserves our very best. I have given some towns in Galilee to pay off King Hiram. He was a great ally to King David and continues to be agreeable in my dealings with him. He was interested in obtaining trade routes through Arabia, Mesopotamia and Egypt. In fact, I am to be married to Pharaoh's daughter from Egypt soon as a gift in one of my political dealings."

Bathsheba playfully hit her son's arm. "That is wonderful news. Congratulations! I shall have a daughter in law! When is the wedding?"

Solomon laughed. "Negotiations are still going on. I am here to show you the temple and there is more to see. Come, can you walk the stairs? There is a better view from the second floor." Bathsheba took her son's hand and let him help her up the stairs. She looked down on the workers below.

"Look at the commotion! They remind me of the ant hills you were fascinated with as a boy. Everyone working so diligently."

"We are actually standing in one of the store rooms. It will help to house the spoils of war, additional materials for repairs if necessary and such. behind us are the stables where the sacrificial animals are kept. The walls are laid with gold."

Bathsheba covered her eyes with one hand as she followed where Solomon was pointing. "They are indeed gold! So bright as they reflect the sun's rays! I bet you will be able to see this temple for miles around."

"The curtain shall hang there." Solomon pointed. "I am having the tapestry made of blue, purple and prison design on thick linen twelve inches thick! The artist have carved the walls with cherubim, palm trees . . ."

Bathsheba interrupted him. "Are those stones?"

Solomon chuckled. "Yes, mother. In the carvings are also turquoise, marble, onyx . . .the men have been working five years. It is almost finished."

"When do you think it will be dedicated?"

"I am hoping within twenty months or so . . . three more barley harvests should see God's magnificent temple complete."

"Those pillars!" Bathsheba called out as she spied two massive pillars holding the roof.

"Made of bronze." Solomon said proudly. "I have actually named them. Jachin is on the right and Boaz is the left column."

"Why?" Bathsheba crinkled her nose and Solomon couldn't help but touch his finger to her nose as he would a young child.

"Because the names mean something. Jachin means "He will establish" or "He gives certainty." Boaz means "by strength." Together they stand to remind Israel that God establishes His nation by His strength and it will certainly continue forth for all generations."

Bathsheba smiled. "You have thought of every detail. What is that?" Solomon pointed to her gaze. "This large basin is called the sea. It will hold seventeen thousand gallons of water for ceremonial washings. I had the artists create what looks like a bowl on the back of a dozen bronze oxen."

"I see that you are building a home for yourself as well?" Bathsheba asked. Solomon smiled and shrugged. "God's house comes first. As soon as this is finished, then yes, I am constructed a home for myself and my new wife. I am gathering materials and the plans have been drawn. Not as mighty as this house, but it is as it should be. God's house should shine above all else." Solomon sighed. "I can scarcely wait for the Ark of the Covenant to be brought here to rest permanently. There will be a dedication service."

"What will you say?"

Solomon set his eyes out at the horizon. "I will tell all of Israel whose hand has fulfilled what He promised to my father David. Since God brought our ancestors out of Egypt he had now home. My father wanted it to be so and God promised him it would be done and here it is! I may sit on the throne of Israel as God promised and I have built the house for the name of the Lord in which to bring the Ark, but it is He who redeemed this people and calls them His own. There is no God like him. Keeping His covenant with his people all these years. It is my prayer that the Lord may hear our honest thanksgiving and the supplications of his servant. Whether there is famine or plenty, defeat or victory, affliction or health. Our God reigns."

"Amen!" Bathsheba wrapped a thin arm around the waist of her son.

CHAPTER TWENTY EIGHT

Bathsheba watched her son from her vantage point on the porch of her chamber. Unlike his father, King David, Solomon reigned in a time of peace among the neighboring nations. The wisdom he had prayed for was given to him abundantly and he became known in the land as a just and reasonable monarch. Far below, he was communicating with his advisors. The folds of his robe gently waving as his hand pointed this way and that as he gave instruction. Bathsheba couldn't hear what they were saying, but took note of the respect in the eyes of his men.

She lifted her gaze a bit farther in the distance as one of the servants walked a horse toward the stables. Solomon's stables were extensive; a construction project that was unprecedented in any other kingdom. The servant was young, only a boy really, as he humbly led the animal to it's stall for grooming. The whinny of horses could be heard. Solomon's herd began from an imported shipment from Egypt procured as bartering material to other kings at their summit meetings. The herd had grown impressively large and required many servants and buildings to maintain. Bathsheba's smile turned down a bit as she considered this. What did the Torah teach? Many years ago, Jehovah called his people out of Egypt never to return, lest they be influenced by their polytheistic beliefs. Would the horses ever give cause for Egyptians to lure the heart of their King Solomon?

Bathsheba turned from her window and continued to ponder. And with all of the polytheistic beliefs, it brought to mind another worry. Her son had recently celebrated the marriage of yet another wife. What was this, 150? 162? Bathsheba had lost count. She remembered being brought into David's household as a wife and the tension of finding her place. But David's women could be counted on her fingers. Her son's harem grew as numerous as his herd of horses! Her heart felt for these women and the pang she felt was true concern for the heart of her son. Was it remaining steadfast?

A maidservant entered her quarters and bowed. "Excuse me, my mistress. Do you require anything?" Bathsheba looked up, and smiled warmly at the girl.

"Thank you, Miriam. I am fine." She thought for a moment as the girl paused at the doorway. "Miriam, tell me."

"Yes, my mistress?"

"What do you think of your king, Solomon, my son?"

"Ma'am?"

Bathsheba shrugged searching her mind for what she really wanted to know. "Is he fair? Well liked among the servants and those of his wives?"

"Yes, ma'am."

Bathsheba motioned for her to come join her on the bench where she sat. A warm breeze waifed in from the nearby window. Haltingly, the girl strode over to where Bathsheba was and nervously curtsied before sitting. Her eyes never lifted high enough to meet Bathsheba's gaze. Bathsheba reached out and stroked her shaking palm.

"Speak freely. I search for a truthful response."

"Yes . . . well, my lord . . . er, King Solomon . . . seems to be graciously blessed by your god."

"How so?" Bathsheba prompted.

"I am often called upon to assist my mother and the kitchen staff for banquets of many visiting rulers. My brother, Samuel works diligently with the mares in the stables and consider myself fortunate to be in your service, dear queen."

Bathsheba patted her hand maternally and thanked her. With a nod, she rose and left the room quickly. Bathsheba sighed. She had good servants but few friends. She returned to the window and tucked a whip of hair that was dancing in the breeze behind her ear. She looked toward the stables again and pastures where many horses were grazing. Her mind drifted to the many chariots and carriages her son had at his disposal. His God-given wisdom had made him prosperous in his trading and commerce.

His wealth included quantities of ivory, exotic animals, fleet of ships at his beckoning in the harbor. Silver, gold, spices, linens, art . . . the tributes he received from visiting dignitaries were exquisite and vast. Was it worth it? She put her gaze below her window where she had seen Solomon speaking with his advisors. They were gone. She turned and left her quarters in search of her son. She asked many of the servants she saw in the palace as to his location and found him writing in one of his many scrolls in one of his official meeting chambers. Guards stood at the door to whom she respectfully bowed and asked for an audience with the king. Patiently she waited outside as the message was relayed to him and nodded to the guards again when she was permitted entrance.

"Mother!" Solomon greeted her with outstretched arms. The folds of his robe swaying with his movements. "I pray that the Lord has kept you well?"

Bathsheba nodded and sank into a nearby chair. "God is good. My body is growing frail with the age of a women who has lived much, but I do not complain. Thank you for seeing me. How are you?"

"Well!" Solomon chuckled and returned to his scroll that he had been writing on. Pointing excitedly, he continued, "Mother, I had my best architects draw up the most beautiful plans for a temple. A great percentage of taxes have gone toward some of the most beautiful materials. We have had cedar wood floated down the Tigris from Lebanon . . . it has the most beautiful grain in it that will make the temple so luxurious."

Bathsheba smiled. How David had wanted to build the temple for God. But she remembered how God had told him that he was a man of war. A man of blood. God's temple would not be built by such a man and David had to be content with the fact that he was to gather the materials but would never see the temple built. That honor would go to their son, Solomon. And here he was, making it a reality.

"Have you begun construction? I have heard no noise of that." Bathsheba asked.

Solomon grinned like he had a secret. "I asked the stones from the quarry already be prepared before delivery here so that the iron tools of hammering nor axe would be heard. I envision the temple to just appear and be as glorious as the God to which I am seeking to honor with a permanent place for the Ark of the Covenant. Unlike our ancestors who had a portable tabernacle, the temple of our Jehovah shall sit on Mount Moriah so that the entire land will know that our God sits highest in my heart."

"You have many scrolls there. What are the other drawings?" Bathsheba asked.

Solomon waved his hand flippantly. "Ah . . . other temples to lesser gods that will be built further down the mountain and nowhere near as luxurious." Bathsheba's brow furrowed. "Other temples? To who?"

Solomon seemed to sit up a bit straighter and his face turned from excitement to a man who was preparing to put her in her place. "I shall honor Sidonia by building a temple to the goddess Ashtoreth, the queen of heaven. I will honor my Ammonite wives with a temple to the bull-god, Molek . . . ."

"How could you?" Bathsheba, forgetting her submission. "Molek is Hebrew for king! And Ashtoreth is a female diety the Egyptians consider as high as Baal himself! We know that there is only one God, the God of Abraham, Isaac, and Jacob . . ."

"That is why I am building the most elaborate temple on the highest mountain to Him!" Solomon interrupted. "Why are so you worried about the other temples? They are just buildings for the people in my land to worship as they wish."

Bathsheba rose, her small frame shaking a bit. "Your father David is not a man after God's own heart by such compromise! I spent the morning looking over your wealth that God has blessed you with. Riches beyond compare! The wisdom you have prayed for. Peace in your land! Why, why my son would you settle for other gods being acknowledged, let alone *worshipped* in your realm?"

"Sit down, mother." Solomon sternly commanded. Dutifully, Bathsheba sank bank into her chair and breathed in slowly.

"Just because I have the temples in the land, does not mean that I will permit some of their practices. There will be no human sacrifices to illustrate that our God . . ."

" . . . is just one of many." Bathsheba hissed. "You can't pick and choose how you will follow the Lord our God! You must obey! The Torah tells us of Abraham's nephew Lot. How he chose to live near Sodom, then within the city walls and then his wife did not escape God's horrible judgement on the land! Compromise will lead to your down fall, my son! I beg you to reconsider."

"God knows my heart is His. I have told you He sits highest in my heart and His temple will reside highest in my land!"

"Your land!" Bathsheba said incredulously. "Who do you think gave this land to you? Out of all your father's sons, who permitted *you* to sit on this throne over your brothers? God himself through the prophet Nathan has chosen you by His grace and for His glory. What a foolish boy are you to think that you can decide what to do with that abundance. It is the worst type of extravagance to be so blasé about His holiness!"

"I am no longer a boy! I may be your son, but I am also your king and you may not counter me any longer!" Solomon's guards drew closer at the sound of their master's voice rising. "You are dismissed!" Then men were suddenly at either side of the chair where Bathsheba sat. Quietly she rose and allowed herself to be escorted to the door. She paused here and turned to see her son once again bent over his scrolls of many temples. In the depths of her being she knew that this would ignite God's anger.

"My son, please hear my last words of advise as I leave your presence. You yourself have said that 'Riches do not profit in the day of wrath. Righteousness delivers from death.' Oh, dear son, please remember the words of the Lord and do not deceive yourself. You are a blessed man indeed. Blessed beyond measure. But do not store up for yourself judgement. Keep your heart humble and teachable as your father David did and you will reap the Lord's richest blessings all your days."

Solomon threw the quill down and smirked at her. "Look around you, mother. I *have* reaped the richest blessings of the Lord. His ways are within me and I will listen to your chatter no more!" With a dismissive wave of his hand, his guards took hold of her elbows and led her from the room.

Back in her chamber, Bathsheba cried and prayed for her son.

CHAPTER TWENTY NINE

The morning lark chirped it's greeting and Bathsheba rubbed her eyes. Groaning, she sat up in her bed and paused for a moment. The years had caused her body to grow weary, eyes dim. An attendant who had been silently standing at the doorway, noticed Bathsheba awaken and had moved to her side. Offering her hand, she helped Bathsheba to stand.

"Thank you." Bathsheba murmured and motioned to the table sitting by the window. It had already been prepared with cheeses, figs and dates. She nibbled on a bit of goat cheese as the servant poured her some milk.

"What time is it?"

"She will be here within the hour." The servant assured her. Bathsheba nodded. She had been looking forward to this day. She watched the city grow with life out her window. God had blessed Jerusalem with another day.

She rose and shuffled to the basin to wash her hands and splash some water on her face. She rubbed her hands on the cool porcelain and wondered where Solomon had acquired such opulence for her. Her attendants had just helped her into a fresh tunic when a servant appeared at her chamber door.

"She is here!"

Bathsheba waved with her hand. "Show her in."

Tamar appeared in the doorway. She stood confidant and had grown into a graceful woman. "Bathsheba!"

"Tamar!" The two women embraced. "It has been so long, thank you for making the journey to see me."

"It has been awhile, just I wanted to make sure to see you before . . ." Tamar's voice trailed off. The two women sat at the table and Bathsheba offered her some breakfast from the plate of fruit and cheese. The servants bustled about around them, pouring Tamar a glass of milk and making the bed.

"I am advanced in years." Bathsheba chuckled. "It is okay to call it what it is."

Tamar took Bathsheba's withered hands in hers. "It is *so* good to see you. I wanted to thank you."

"Thank me?"

"All those years ago, when I left Jerusalem in shame." Tamar looked down at her hands now resting in her lap. "My mother did not know how to comfort me, Absolom had avenged my honor by killing Amnon . . .so much heartache. I had to flee. I was thankful that I was not to be punished, but who would have me? I was no longer pure. But you. . ." Tamar looked lovingly into her eyes. "You believed in me. You showed love to me, even though I wasn't your daughter."

Bathsheba patted her cheek. "You were always like a daughter to me."

Tamar's eyes filled with tears. Her eyes drifted to the hairbrush nearby and darted to grab it. "May I?"

Bathsheba smiled and nodded. Tamar lovingly stood behind her and began to brush Bathsheba's grey hair. Her delicate fingers working through the curls, gently detangling them as she began to speak.

"I went to Joppa to be near the sea. I enjoyed the fresh air and being in a city where no one knew my name. I called myself 'Tabitha.'

"Aramaic for gazelle." Bathsheba replied.

"Yes. I chose a name that sounded beautiful and graceful, all the things I wanted to be but didn't feel on the inside. The townspeople assumed I was a widow and a dear family took me in. I helped with the household chores, the cooking, watching the children. . . and then I met him."

"Him?"

Tamar stopped brushing her hair and sat down across from her so she could look into Bathsheba's eyes.

"Josiah. He is a longshoreman at the Joppa harbor. He would unload the ships as they came in with their exotic cargo. Fabrics, construction materials, spices, animals . . ." Tamar popped an olive into her mouth and stood. She leaned her hands on the window sill and looked out across Jerusalem.

"Josiah means Yahweh heals. Don't you think that is appropriate? God healed me from a terrible injustice and purified me. So now I truly feel like a new person . . . a 'Tabitha."

"The name suits you." Bathsheba encouraged. "And Josiah? That sounds like the God we serve . . . One who restores."

Tamar turned and looked at Bathsheba. "We were married this past spring."

Bathsheba clapped her hands in delight. "That is wonderful, Tamar!"

"He is so handsome!" She gushed. "With unloading the ships, he has such powerful arms and yet is so gentle when he wraps me up in them." Tamar stroked her hand on her belly. "And we are expecting our first child!"

Bathsheba waved her hands in the air excitedly and giggled. "When?"

"Next harvest. How I wish you could be there."

Bathsheba shook her head. Traveling was too difficult now and her time was short. Tamar grew silent, knowing what Bathsheba was thinking. She came and gently knelt at Bathsheba's feet and placed her head in Bathsheba's lap. Bathsheba stroked Tamar's dark chestnut hair.

"Did you know that my brother Absolom named his daughter Tamar after me?" she got lost in a wispy memory for a moment and grew silent. "If this child is a girl, we wish to name her Bathsheba." Tamar said quietly.

"Child of the oath."

Tamar looked up at her quizzically. "What?"

Bathsheba smiled. "That is what my name means; daughter of the oath. My father never quite told me what oath exactly, but I always thought that my name produced an air of hope."

"Oh, that is quite true. You gave me hope when I had none. You reminded me of how God sees me." Tamar stood and twirled in a circle. "And look at me now! Married, with child, living in the beautiful harbor town of Joppa."

Bathsheba beamed. "Jehovah is a good God. It really means the world to me that you came to see me."

"I shall never forget you. May God's richest blessings be upon you, Bathsheba." Tamar smiled.

"Oh, child, He already has. I have been abundantly blessed with years. Seeing my grandchildren, wife of a king and the mother of a king!" Bathsheba stopped short and did not mention the name of her first husband, Uriah but her heart fluttered in her reverie and she could not help but think of him. "We have not had an easy life, you and I." She told Tamar. "But God was there, working in our every day. Teach your child of His ways. Grow her up in His commandments."

Tamar promised to and kissed Bathsheba's knobby knuckles. Bathsheba watched her disappear from her chamber and looked back out over the city of David. She nodded to herself. Yes, God had been gracious and healed her just like he had Tamar. She hoped the historians would remember her as a woman of integrity. She knew that her lineage and life had been chronicled by the royal scribes. She desired their words to be kind.

The annals of scripture continue to record the legacy of Israel, God's chosen people. Bathsheba marveled at how God had woven all the circumstances of her life into such a powerful testimony of His faithfulness. He had taken a maid from a small southern tribe in Israel and brought her to Jerusalem be a Queen. He had replaced her sadness and tragedy with accolades and exultations. He had echoed this in the life of her step-daughter, Tamar who now saw herself as Tabitha; a new creation. Jehovah further blessed Bathsheba by allowing her to see her son Solomon rise to succeed his father King David on the throne. She witnessed the construction of God's holy temple that Israel had long waited for and saw how Solomon prospered.

Solomon's God-given wisdom had helped him make sound decisions with commerce and trading, using his vast fleet of ships to bring merchandise from the most remotest of nations. Dignitaries from all over like the famed Queen of Sheba traveled to meet this unique king and would lavish gifts upon him; exotic animals, jewels and large quantities of gold. The Jewish historian Josephus would record on Solomon's extraordinary wealth and great reputation throughout the land. It was also said, however, that Solomon imposed heavy taxation and his judgements grew clouded with the enormous influence of his harem and fame.

Bathsheba was laid to rest with her forefathers long before she ever knew that her son Solomon was perhaps the wealthiest man who has ever lived. Gold, silver, ivory, animals, slaves, investments, spices, gems, garments, armor, armies, palaces, wives, children. . . .but it was Solomon himself that would always esteem his wisdom as the greatest treasure to hold. Recognizing that wisdom only comes from God Himself, Solomon felt it was necessary to write down what he understood and to pass this wealth on to others for their benefit. The result is now known and read as the book of Proverbs and Ecclesiastes.

"Happy is the man who finds wisdom. For her proceeds are better than all profits of silver, and her gain is much finer than gold. Everything else is meaningless, utterly meaningless. What do people gain from all their labors at which they toil under the sun? Generations come and generations go but the earth remains forever. What has been will be again . . . for there is nothing new under the sun."

CPSIA information can be obtained
at www.ICGtesting.com
Printed in the USA
LVHW010845010719
622841LV00003B/530